PRIMA MATERIA
w r i t i n g s
volume 2   2 0 0 3

Home, Family, and Other Mixed Blessings

☽

Short Fiction by Writers
from the Hudson Valley, New York

Edited by Brent Robison

Bliss Plot
PRESS

Prima Materia
Volume 2, 2003

Acknowledgment:
"Family Man" by Brent Robison originally appeared in *Crania*, an online literary journal at www.crania.com.

Published by Bliss Plot Press, PO Box 68, Mt. Tremper, NY 12457
Editor/Publisher: Brent Robison
Associate Publisher: Wendy Klein

For subscription information, inquire at the address above or by e-mail at primamateria@brentrobison.com.

Submissions: Unsolicited manuscripts should include a self-addressed, stamped envelope (SASE) or an e-mail address; otherwise we cannot respond. For submission guidelines, send an SASE with your request, or visit www.brentrobison.com.

ISBN 0-9718908-1-1
ISSN 1538-9553

Printed in the United States of America

Cover design by Brent Robison
Photo: "The Silent Mansion" © Brent Robison, 1997

To find the philosopher's stone:
"Pray, read, read, read, read again, labor, and discover."
—*Mutus Liber*
(Wordless Book)
1677

The Hudson River Valley

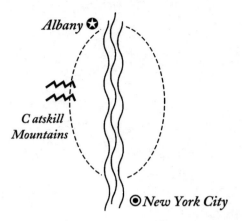

In 1609, Henry Hudson sailed the Half Moon up the river that would one day bear his name. He called it the River of Mountains and wrote of its valley, "It is as pleasant a land as one can tread upon." Washington Irving later made local folk tales famous with "The Legend of Sleepy Hollow" and "Rip Van Winkle," capturing a dark magic that most certainly hides in these hills. A surprising number of arts colonies and spiritual retreats have found refuge in these wooded valleys for over a century. Today, rumor has it that the region claims more "artists" per capita than any comparable area in the country. And UFOs as well.

With "The City," the center of the world, just an easy jaunt downriver, and world-class culture swarming north to our doorstep, we can still enjoy the sight of a black bear eating berries in the backyard. There's something in the air here, or the soil, or the water. There's an energy in the Hudson Valley that has called creative spirits from all over the world. There's serious talent here, working in secret in these woods and river towns. This book gives a sampling of the stories we have to tell.

Prima Materia
Volume 2   2003

---------------- ☾ **Contents** ☽ ----------------

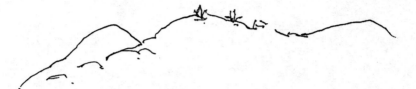

Art is the lie that tells the truth better than the truth does.

—*Chuck Palahniuk*

Horizons While Hiking
Carol Field

))) ————————————————————————————

Introduction

In early 2002, on a similar frigid, sleeting night, I sat in the same cozy, firelit room that I'm sitting in now, writing the introduction to the debut issue of Prima Materia. Then, I had no idea what would happen next. Would the book really come out? Would people like it? In the months since, I've discovered that the answer to both questions is "Yes!" Or even: "Of course; what are you worried about?" As a novice to the world of editing and publishing, I've learned more in the last few months than can be put down here. I feel privileged to be able to go another round on this adventure.

Welcome! The second issue of Prima Materia is an entirely different journey from the first: new voices, new visions, new themes. It's a solid array of mature, thoughtful, tightly crafted, well-developed narratives, in styles both experimental and traditional.

This volume is called "Home, Family, and Other Mixed Blessings" because, once again, a connective thread appeared organically. As the strongest stories made themselves known from among the multitude of submissions, I was surprised to see that many (not all) of them shared the same power source: the pain and joy we feel toward those odd strangers who fill our living rooms, kitchens, bedrooms, and back yards. Here are common domestic environments into which new, clear light is being cast. The characters' struggles take place squarely within the context of being husbands and wives, parents, children, brothers and sisters, people living with people...and in a couple of cases, even the house itself takes a leading role.

In a wider sense, these stories tell us about living in America, in the world, in the state of being human: how do we find what's important in this national home, this global family, this stew of spiritual and material pursuits? Is loving each other all, finally, that we can do? Is there another dimension beyond this one we see? Good fiction doesn't prescribe neat answers; just asking the questions is contribution enough, because no answer is sufficient anyway.

I'm confident that there are stories here that will resonate with you. After all, we're all in the same fix, aren't we? As Greg Brown sings:

> *Everyone is scared, everyone's alone*
> *Unless hand reach for hand when the trouble comes*
> *All around the world when the dark night falls*
> *We should be sitting around the fire telling stories**

I hope you enjoy Prima Materia!

> —*Brent Robison*
> *November 2002*
> *Mt. Tremper, NY*

**Greg Brown, "Telling Stories," *Milk of the Moon*, Red House Records, 2002

PRIMA MATERIA
w r i t i n g s

Home, Family, and Other Mixed Blessings

☽

Donald Ray Gilman

)) ————————————————

My Panther

1. Sam

No matter what foster home I was in, Sam could find me. He would always pull up in a different Cadillac. He'd walk up through the front door of the house and into the living room like he owned the place.

"Where's my boy?"

No foster parent ever uttered a word of protest. He was Sam McCarroll.

"Goddammit, ain't these assholes feedin' ya, boy? C'mere an' hug Grampa Sam's neck."

And the ritual would begin.

"Grampa's got something for ya, boy."

He reached into his pocket and pulled out a fresh, crisp dollar bill.

"You want a dollar?"

I'd nod yes with head and shoulders.

"Well now, only a man earns a dollar. You a man?"

"Yessir."

"Well, you gonna have to prove it to me. See that wall over there? Go butt your head against that wall like a man."

I walked over and proceeded to address the wall. I butted my head against it. It made a dull thud.

"Hell, boy! I seen little girls butt walls harder'n that. You a little girl? Then git your tail over there and butt that wall like a man."

This time I stepped into the blow like a boxer. Putting the full force of my seventy-five pounds into it. This thud had resonance.

I looked over my shoulder for his approval.

"That's better, boy. But you ain't hit it like a man yet."

He began to fold the bill and place it back in his pocket.

"PawPaw! PawPaw! I am a man. I'll show you."

I turned and faced the wall once again. With a couple of skipping jumps I crossed the room and butted the wall. There was a solid deep BOOM and I staggered back a few feet.

"Yeee Haaa! Now that's how a man butts a wall, son. You jes' earned yourself a dollar."

With great pride I walked towards him to collect my reward.

As I reached for it he pulled it back and leaned into my face.

"That's how a man butts a wall. Now show me how a *McCarroll* man butts that goddamn wall."

His breath was in my face for a second as I took in his eyes.

Then I turned and ran at full gallop across the room, charging the wall like an enraged bull.

BOOOOOMMMM!

A piece of sheetrock came off and stuck to my forehead. The divot it left in the wall was shaped like one of those little dogs that dance on a ball in the circus.

Sam's upside down face was smiling down my prone body.

"You a McCarroll, son," he whispered. "Don't you ever forget it."

As the dollar floated down on me, I could hear the screen door slam, his boots cross the porch, and the V-8 roar on the Caddy.

God, I loved that son of a bitch.

2. Charlie

Amyna bird looks like a crow but it can talk like a parrot. With the exception of the fact that a myna bird can actually sound exactly like the person that teaches it to speak. My grandfather, Sam, gave my grandmother a myna bird. *Charlie*, she called it.

He gave it to her when I was six.

My grandmother loved animals. When Sam wasn't in jail he was a used car salesman. When someone couldn't pay he would occasionally take an animal as partial payment.

The day he brought Charlie home I think he was trying to make up for the fact that he had refused to let my grandmother return to teaching, the job she had and loved before they married.

He came through the door, all six-foot-four of him and said, "Goddammit, Jesse, you wanna teach somethin'? Teach this goddamned bird to talk."

I was between foster homes and staying with them for the summer. I watched her spend hours trying to teach Charlie to speak.

"Pretty bird, pretty bird," she would say, and "Think of that. Think of that."

One night Sam came home drunk, which always made him meaner than he normally was. I was sitting beside my grandmother.

With one ape-like swing of Sam's arm, Charlie's cage went flying... and so did my grandma. As she struggled to get to her knees, he moved around the coffee table.

"Goddammit Jesse, you been playin' with this goddamned bird all day and ain't made me no supper?"

Gramma had one of those rotary dial phones, the kind that had real bell ringers inside. It clanged loudly as he hit her square in the face with it. Her mouth split open and my grandma's blood and spit landed on my shirt.

7

By this time she was on her back and her skirt had flown up around her waist. As she struggled to get up, Sam started at her again. He was preparing to kick her with the alligator cowboy boots he'd bought in Corpus Christi.

I threw myself on top of her. I spread my body across my grandma and prayed.

"Please Jesus, don't let my Grampa kill my Gramma. Please Jesus, don't let my Grampa kill my Gramma...."

Over and over again with my eyes squeezed so tight I saw colors. When I finally gathered the courage to open my eyes, Sam was gone.

My grandma's face was open...peeled open...just teeth and a tongue, trying to say, "Are you all right, Donnyray?"

Charlie's cage was on its side and as he walked, it rolled across the floor. I called the Sheriff.

"Well Jesse, you know how Sam can git," he said as the ambulance doors closed.

A week later Sam died when his truck leapt a curve running from a State Trooper after a bar fight. He was sixty-seven years old. Gramma and I never talked about it.

Charlie lived for sixteen years after that.

"Think of that. Think of that." And "Pretty bird. Pretty bird." he would say in the sweet soft tones of my grandmother. And every once in a while he would say, "Goddammit Jesse, where's my supper?"

3. Gramma

My grandmother gave me a panther when I was little. He was eight feet tall standing on his hind legs, and his coat was as black as a pit.

I was between foster homes and I woke up in the middle of the night screaming. Gramma Jesse came into the bedroom.

"Donnyray, what's the matta honey?"

"Bad dream, bad dream," I said as I stuck my hands in my armpits and rocked back in forth in the bed.

"Well, Gramma Jesse can take care of that," she said as she left the room. In a second she came back in the room with a large chalkboard. I remember thinking I was too big for it because it had the alphabet across the top and the numbers 1 to 10 across the bottom and I knew all that stuff. She placed it on the bed and against the wall. Her wrinkled fingers picked up a piece of chalk from the tray at the bottom and she made a long, sweeping curved line. Then she made another and another. The motion of her arm reminded me of a man I had seen conducting an orchestra on TV. Soon the lines became a fierce, beautiful panther, poised on a tree limb with his haunches in the air as if he were about to leap down and attack something.

With a flourish she put the chalk back in the tray.

"Now, what's his name?" she asked me.

"Treat," I said for no apparent reason.

"Well, Treat here's a hunter. You know what he eats now, don'tcha?"

I looked at her, a little afraid of the answer, and shook my head no.

"He eats bad dreams. He's your panther and he's gon' watch over you from now on when you sleepin'. He gon' see dem bad dreams comin', jump off dat limb, chase 'em ol' bad dreams down like dey a jackrabbit and gobble'em up."

She tickled me with the "gobble'em up" part and I let out a belly laugh. Then without missing a beat she picked up the eraser and in a few quick motions, my panther was gone.

I sat there with my mouth open staring at my grandmother's face beaming down on me.

"Why?" I stuttered.

"Cause now *you* gon' draw Treat. I'm gonna show you how so he can be there whenever you need 'im."

She placed the chalk in my hand and my hand in hers. We made a line…and then another and another. At some point she let go of my hand and guided me in hushed sweet whispers, until there he was again. My panther. Only in some way I couldn't yet understand, better than he was before. I was in awe of what I'd done.

I looked up at her face as if to ask her a question but nothing came out.

"That's one fine panther you got there, Donnyray. Yessirree Bob. That's one fine panther."

Irene McGarrity

)) ─────────────────────────

Beautiful Track and Field Stars

There was a knock at the door and Sera pulled the covers up over her head. She left a little opening by her ear so she wouldn't suffocate. So there would be enough light. She was right in the middle of a book her mother had left on the back of the toilet. Sera didn't want to stop. She went on reading:

> Wilma moved down the dark hallway with the
> grace of a woman and the curiosity of a cat.

The book fell out of her hands and onto her face. She could smell the pages. They smelled like something she wanted to remember but couldn't. She smelled harder. She breathed in the pages and all the words on them, but still Sera couldn't remember. It was something. Something about cats maybe. She took the book off of her face and studied the cover in the little bit of light her bed cave gave her. There was a man with big muscles and long hair and a woman with a white dress on. They were making out. Sera flipped back to the page she had been reading. She thought, if she had designed the cover, she would have given them both cat heads instead of human heads. And they wouldn't be making out. They would be sailing on a ship or going on a ride at Great Adventure. It would be much more interesting, she thought. All of those people screaming and running away when they saw the cat people on Free Fall. Dropping their popcorn and hot dogs. Throwing their cotton candy on the ground so they could run faster. Making out just wasn't that interesting. Sera couldn't understand why it was in almost every book her mother left on the back of the toilet. It was something she had never done and could never imagine doing. She didn't understand how people could go from having a conversation or laughing or walking or eating or doing all sorts of normal things, to moving their tongues around in each other's mouths. She thought maybe it had something to do with boredom. Whenever she thought about making out, she imagined two people sitting on a couch, staring at a television set, smoking cigarettes and drinking coffee. They would take turns yawning and sighing and eventually, one of them would ask the other one, "You wanna make out?" But there were so many other things to do. Why make out?

She had tried it once a long time ago, just to see what it was all about. She had climbed up on her father's lap and hung her arms around his neck. She said, "Daddy, you wanna make out?"

He didn't answer. He just kept stuttering. "Sera, I— you—I mean we can't—."

That's when her mother cut in. She said, "Go to your room. You are a very fresh young lady." So Sera had gone to her room and stared at the wall. She didn't know anything more about making out but figured it wasn't worth the trouble. It certainly wasn't worth making her mother mad.

Sera smelled the pages and there was another knock at the door. She pretended that it was part of the story:

> Wilma took light, careful steps, yet her steps were persistent and steady. *There was a knock at the door, but Wilma was so intent on getting to the end of that hallway so she could find the guy from the cover and make out with him again, that she didn't even hear it.*

Sera lifted up the covers. The air supply was getting tight in her bed cave. The smell of the pages was taking over. What was it? Old people? The ocean? She breathed deeply a few times and then went back inside the cave. Wilma was almost at the end of the hallway:

> And with each step, her heart beat a little faster. Her mind raced like a beautiful runner on a track, muscles tense, sweating, out of breath. And there was something else happening. A stirring inside of her that she had never felt before, but that she believed she would always feel from that day on. *Then, suddenly, her head exploded and a new one emerged from her neck, replacing it. Only it wasn't the head of a woman at all. It was the head of a cat. Oh how tragic! Now that guy from the cover would never want to make out with her. Wilma feared he could never love a mutant like her.*

Sera laughed and when there was another knock at the door, she pretended it was just an echo in her bed cave. She kept reading:

> Wilma could see that the light was on in the room at the end of the hallway; there was a space at the bottom of the door, which had allowed some of the light to escape. Wilma was drawn to it, like a bee to honey, like a moth to a flame, *like a cat to a litter box.*

Sera's eyes drifted from her book to the ceiling of her cave and she remembered the smell. She had smelled it the day before her mother had gotten rid of her cat Fluffy. It seemed like a normal day at first. Sera had been in her bed cave, reading like usual. And the same thing had happened. The book had fallen on her face. That was when Sera heard the first scream. She didn't get up right away because for some reason, she thought it had come from the book. From the woman on the cover who looked almost exactly like Wilma only her name was Natasha. Sera had said, "What's wrong, Natasha?" Then there was another scream and she knew it was her mother. Sera dropped the book and ran down stairs. She looked at her father, who was sitting on the couch reading the paper. He looked up at her. "Was that your mother?" he said. And they both ran down to the basement together. That was where the screams were coming from. Her mother was at the bottom of the steps with the kitty litter scoop in her hand. She screamed again when she saw them. Sera's father said, "What is it? What's the matter?"

Her mother was shaking and crying. One thing that Sera noticed was that her mother didn't really look scared. She looked angry.

"What?" said her father. "What is it, Nora?" Finally, after a lot of crying and probing and trembling and melodrama, Sera's mother choked out, "There's dead mice in there. At least ten of them." And she pointed to the litter box with the scoop like it was part of her hand. Like she couldn't let it go. Sera looked at a dark lump on the floor by her mother's foot. It looked like a cat turd. But when she looked at it more closely, she saw the whiskers and the tail. She could see its little ears. Then Sera saw Fluffy. He was in the other corner of the basement where his toys were. He was licking himself. "Bad Fluffy," said her dad. "You are a bad cat."

The next day, Fluffy was gone. Sera looked all over for him. She looked outside, in the bushes, in the garage, in the kitchen cabinets where he hid sometimes. She looked under her parents' bed and in all the bedrooms. Fluffy was nowhere. It was like he had never been there at all. Sera went into the living room.

Her parents were sitting in front of the television, smoking cigarettes and drinking coffee, *on the verge of making out, no doubt.* "Where's Fluffy? I can't find him anywhere. Have you seen him?"

Neither one of them answered her right away. Her father looked down into his coffee cup as if Fluffy might be floating around in there somewhere. Her mother took a drag from her cigarette and looked at Sera. She shook her head and looked away. "There was something really wrong with that cat." She turned her eyes back to Sera. "It's not normal for a cat to want to keep dead mice in a litter box."

Sera noticed the look on her mother's face was the same, but without all the screaming and shaking. She still looked angry. "But where is he?"

Her mother said, "It's just not healthy to have a cat like that around."

Sera ran down stairs to the basement and saw that the litter box was gone. All of Fluffy's little cat toys were packed up in a plastic bag where the litter box had been. There was a piece of tape on the bag that said, "donation" in black marker. That was one thing about Sera's mother; she always labeled things.

There was another knock and Sera came down from the ceiling of the cave, back to Wilma, the cat woman:

> *Wilma knocked at the door, but there was no answer so she* let herself into the room, as quiet as a mouse, and there, sitting before the fire place, was the most glorious creature she had ever seen. *He too was a cat person, but the sight of this did not scare or disgust her. He was beautiful and strange. He looked almost majestic sitting in the red, velvet chair. She no longer felt like a mutant; she was finally able to see her own beauty in him. His fur was thick and luxurious. His whiskers, firm, but yielding*

to her touch.   She stroked him and he immediately began to purrrrrrrrrrrrr.

Sera's bedroom door opened and she heard her mother's voice. "Sera, it's time to go. Enough is enough."

Sera went deeper into her cave. The air supply was gone. There was only the smell of the pages and that day that her mother had screamed. There wasn't anymore light:

She saw how it wasn't bad at all to be a cat person.   In fact, it was better than being a regular human.   Cats had excellent night vision, perfect for making out.   Wilma and her immaculate lover stroked each other and purred.

"Sera, let's go. Mr. Wallace is waiting." The voice was getting closer and she moved even deeper into her cave:

They started to make out as well as two cat people could.   Their whiskers were gloriously intertwined, like the weaving of a beautiful wicker cat bed, and their rough tongues made music like a maraca and a tambourine and a harmonica going all at once. Wilma felt light, like a rollercoaster swishing through the air.

Then she heard her father's voice. "Pumpkin, it's going to be okay. Come out from under the blanket." The walls of Sera's cave began to collapse and she closed her eyes. She didn't want to see it happen. When she opened her eyes, her mother's hands were on her hips and she had that look on her face again. Sera didn't understand. She didn't understand how her mother could destroy an entire bed cave and then put her hands on her hips. "Let's go now, young lady. Your father has been knocking on your door for twenty minutes. I'm not going to make Mr. Wallace wait anymore."

Her father said, "You can come home as soon as you feel better, pumpkin."

Sera wondered if her mother had put her hands on her hips after she had gotten rid of Fluffy.

"Let's go," she said. "Now." Her mother had a plastic bag in her hand and she was filling it with things from Sera's shelves and her dresser drawers. The bag had a little piece of tape on it that said, "Sera's things" in black magic marker.

Sera sat up and her father took the book out of her hands. He looked at the cover. "Where did you get this?"

She said, "The back of the toilet."

Her mother took it out of his hands and looked at it. Sera hoped she would put it in the plastic bag but she didn't. She held onto it and put her free hand on her hip. Sera's father handed Sera a pair of socks and her sneakers. She put them on, one sock, one sneaker, one sock, one sneaker. She stared at her feet and then looked up at her father.

He smiled. He said, "All ready, pumpkin?" They walked out of her bedroom and down the long hallway that lead to the front door. Sera closed her eyes and pretended to be Wilma. She was beautiful and an expert at making out. Her heart was beating and there were beautiful track and field stars zooming around and around in her head. Only, instead of human track and field stars, they were fast cats. And they purred so loudly that the people in the bleachers had to hold onto each other to keep from falling off. She was on the verge of something big. Mr. Wallace was standing in front of the door. He looked different than he usually did in his office, behind his desk. He was still old with gray hair but his face looked rubbery. Sera stared at him and he smiled a rubbery smile. "Hello Sera." She felt her father's hand holding her elbow carefully, but firmly. She looked back at him and he smiled at her like she was a stranger in a supermarket whose shopping cart he had just accidentally bumped into. But she pretended not to notice. She was Wilma now. Her mother was at her other side, hands still on her hips. Sera was right in front of Mr. Wallace now. He was still smiling his rubbery smile. She thought his face looked like a Halloween mask. "Ready to go?" He asked. She wanted to pull at all that rubber. She wanted to take the mask off and see his real face. But she was Wilma. And Mr. Wallace was the glorious creature she had stumbled upon. He wasn't a rubbery old looking man at all. He was beautiful. Sera took his rubbery face in her hands and started making out with him. The inside of his mouth was warm and wet. It tasted like tuna fish and saltines. She heard her mother scream like she had the day she found the dead mice, and she felt her father's hands trying to pull her away. After a little bit of a struggle, he yanked Sera away from Mr. Wallace and there was sort of a squishy popping sound, like a plunger being pulled out of a toilet bowl.

Her mother's eyes were wide as if Sera's head had exploded and been replaced by a glorious cat head. She said, "God, Sera. God."

Her father didn't say anything. He looked down at the carpet and put his hands behind his back. Mr. Wallace was wiping his rubbery lips with the back of his hand. He was shaking his head, and looking at her like she was bad. Like she had been caught keeping dead things in her bed cave.

~

In the ambulance, she wasn't Wilma anymore. Outside of her bed cave and away from her book from the back of the toilet, she wasn't even Sera anymore. She wasn't anybody. She was something that people were getting rid of. She was as good as all of that popcorn and cotton candy the scared people had thrown away. She was as good as those dead mice in Fluffy's litter box. Her father looked down at her and touched her leg. "It'll be okay, pumpkin. You'll be better in no time." He jumped out and slammed one of the doors shut. The big guy who had strapped

Sera to the stretcher slammed the other one. After a few seconds, the ambulance lurched forward and she heard the gravel of the driveway crunch under the tires. Then there was nothing but smooth road sound and the voices of Mr. Wallace and the big guy talking up front. Sera stared up at the ceiling and then at all the strange things around her. There were all sorts of knobs and metal looking things that didn't make any sense. Sera felt her eyes fill with tears. All she had wanted to do was finish her book:

> *Wilma and her newfound cat lover made out so thoroughly and for such an extended period of time, that their two cat heads became one. In a miraculous flash of light, there remained only a giant cat head, making out with itself. It purred at such a loud volume, that the entire room shook. The passion of Wilma and her lover had created a miraculous and eternal cat head. It was all Wilma had ever wanted, to be part of something so amazing, so pure, so endless. It would be there, in that room, purring and making out for all time.*

Audrey Borenstein

⟨⟨

Tomorrow's Work

Time was up. *Leave the thread dangling, leave off in mid-sentence.*

How warm it was now; the sun had been buttering the crown of her head, the tops of her glasses frames as she sat hunched here writing. And there had been that romp, that steeplechase of the clouds enticing her to fall into the soulsleep of reverie. But her will to work had prevailed; she had remained awake at her loom.

Whole the woman had returned to her, whole and present. She had realized her intention to bring the woman back up from her last underwater swim, to follow through the woman's eyes the breaking of the dawn in the sky beyond her window, there in the nearest dimension, laying bare the leaves of the oak in the parallel universe steeping in the whitegold light bleeding quietly through the curtains she would have drawn across the stare of night. To follow its course over her oval braided rug, its climb up the bedposts. To follow its widening spill upon the woman's figure just now stirring, that was tomorrow's work.

She pulled the windows shut and tidied her desk, carried her tray downstairs, rinsed the dishes. Then she put together her brown bag lunch.

After she locked the front door, she took up the big stick she used to arm herself against the self-appointed four-legged gendarmes of the Village streets. *Mom's shillelagh* Jamie dubbed it, much to his older brother's amusement. In vain she protested to both sons that none of the found objects she made into walking sticks were made of wood tough as the oak for which her father's ancestral town in Ireland was named.

At the memorial stone marking the halfpoint of her journey up the Avenue of the Huguenot, her fellow-citizen's too-clever phrase in last week's *Palatine Post* repeated itself inside her head: *"The artists of our Village suffer from sensory* under*load."* In the protest letter-to-the-editor she'd cast into the bin for recycled papers yesterday was an evocation of one day last March when the sky opened over the Flemish roof of single pitch atop Memorial House and flocks of redpolls streamed through the widening rift. Pied white and tawny sparrow-shapes diving down, alighting to search for weed seeds in the little snow-dusted field beyond the late 17th-century stone house. Winter letting go. Thawing crystals sheathing the catkins of the birches falling drop by drop, acrid smoke from the charcoal pots smoldering in the apple orchards, swarming redpolls riding snow whitecaps on a Macbeth morning in March.

Five of nine. She decided to continue on Huguenot, walking briskly now to the corner. The year she and Jamie had found the way to let one another go she had taken this route, the two opposing camps of her parenthood fighting their last good fight. "Ought you *drive* him away, then, leave him forsaken for the second time?" the one side demanded. "Was it not enough that he lost his father? He'll be forsaken a second time soon enough. Sooner even than that, given the cretins governing most of humanity." But the other side had pounced on this as an evasion of that responsibility she knew was hers alone. To set him free. That he might claim his own life.

And she hers.

"Still a sleepy town, Katele," she heard her long-dead first father-in-law say as she passed the deserted Deli. "Same as when you and the two boys first moved here, remember? They say that the Huguenots used to be up working at the crack of dawn, that's farmers for you. You can do the same, once they're grown."

The kindliness of his shade. Would that all the dead were as benevolent.

Across Oakdale, the Library, her workplace, her livelihood. Almost at her journey's end.

When you first moved here. The abyss of the long years ahead of mothering two half-brothers, her orphaned sons, was opening before her at the time, and her father-in-law's loss was the most grievous that a parent can know. Yet Papa Roth had held out his hand to her. And he had never forsaken her. Even now, from the other world, he came as a father still, breathing courage into her still.

She unlocked the side door of the Library. The Children's Reading Hour would begin at half-past nine. She hurried through the rooms, snapping on the lights as she half-ran to unlock the double Dutch door.

Shadows still sat like persons facing one another on the built-in stone benches on the portico.

In his latest letter, Jamie had written that one of his colleagues told him a true story of a book of poetry so tiny it can be passed through the eye of a needle. Using a microscope, an Eastern European craftsman sewed strands of a spider's web together to make a tiny, twelve-page chapbook. "There's an eight-line text on each of the pages that covers an area of half a square millimeter. This is less than .008 of a square inch! The letters are less than four-thousandths of a millimeter—.00016 of an inch—wide! I thought of *you*, Mom, of the miracle of fierce compression you try to achieve in your writing."

The telephone was ringing.

Jamie, lad. It isn't compression that's miraculous. It's growing the heart strong enough to carry the threads over and under and through these thousands of crossings, it's keeping them alive and whole with this terrible, lumbering patience. It's teaching yourself to till with a tenacity fierce enough to match that of the most violent or severe elements, after your first seeding. This tenacity that feels itself to be half-affliction, half-madness.

She lifted the receiver.

Beyond the bourne, the woman resumed her weaving.

Tania Zamorsky

))

Squid in Love

R amona likes Bruno 'cuz he has three arms.
　　That's right, three.

Right now, *none* of the little boys have cars or clothes or good jobs, and they all have good hair, so it probably seems as good a criterion as any for her to use in her search for a soul mate.

~

Not that my Bruno's a saint; he's as shallow as the next fellow.

Ramona has a giant raspberry, you see, on her nose. It sits right there on the tip, like a tough little crabapple. Or a rose-colored sight on a rifle. From far away, it seems to glow and guide her. It guided her straight to Bruno.

She thinks it makes her special and so does he. You would think it was a ruby or something, the way that girl runs around, waving it, sticking it in everybody else's business. Sometimes, after she makes Bruno chase her for a little while, she surrenders in the corner of the sandbox and lets him touch it. He squeezes it gently, right on the red part, and she lets out a little squeak, like a puppy's chew toy. A chew toy for my three-armed boy.

The reality is that none of the other children will play with them, but Bruno and Ramona don't know that yet. They think they've chosen each other, and chosen well. They're a regular power couple, those two.

~

Of course, Ramona is going to have that raspberry removed.

Neither she nor Bruno is aware of this either, but this is what Ramona's mother has been screaming at me silently, via some kind of telepathic disclaimer, from across the sandbox. And that's okay, I think. *I hear you.* Just let them fall in love for a little while. Just show me where to sign.

She watches, with a pained expression, as our two children play. Her instinct, I know, is to take her daughter and run-away from us, away from my son. And I don't blame her. How does she think *I* felt, I feel like asking her, the first time I watched Bruno play with himself?

But *she* knows that—for the time being, anyway—she and her raspberry-nosed Ramona have no place to go. To drive this point home, to buy Bruno just a little more time, I'll do anything. I have no shame. I'll hum the melody to that song about the reindeer. A few times I do this. I raise my eyebrows and glance over at the other children and then back. To help this other mother understand that her daughter's no big whoop either. To remind her that beggars can't be choosers. To beg her not to go— please not yet, just to stay a little longer—so that Bruno has someone. Besides me.

She's not a bad person, this mother. In fact, she is the closest thing I have, in this competitive little urban playgroup in the park near my house, to a friend. And so we have struck a deal. She stays. Her daughter plays. For now, anyway. With an option to renegotiate terms at a later date.

Trust me; I understand the impulse. It's a scary thing, that arm. Scared my bum husband right out of our lives; not even Bruno could hold him. I thought about running too, lots of times, but whenever I decided that today was the day, that I was ready to go, go figure, I always found myself packing Bruno. I guess that's what mothers do: they pack Bruno.

~

Sometimes a new mother, someone who doesn't know, will join our little circle. Maybe she is trying to escape too. Maybe she will have walked the few extra blocks north, hoping that this sandbox will be different, that no one will know them. That she and her son will be popular.

Seeing my son playing by himself, she will gently push her boy in Bruno's direction. She will think herself kind. You're the big kid on campus now, she'll say. Be big about it and go play with the loser.

But then she'll see It. Bruno and her son will somehow be holding hands, even though Bruno will also be holding two hands out to his side, flapping like an angel's wings.

She will frown, squint, confused. She will think her eyes are playing tricks on her, when really it will only be me.

It's Bruno's penis, I'll tell her, that her hotshot son is holding onto for dear life. "As you might imagine," I'll say, "his father and I are very proud."

But Bruno hates it when I tell that joke. He's warned me that he's going to get a complex, not to mention the other kid, if I keep it up. So he lets go of his new best friend's hand and waves at this woman shyly.

It's a good thing these scenes usually take place in a sandbox, is all I can say. For the other mother's sake. For all of these other mothers who faint at the drop of a hat. Or the mere wave of fifteen little fingers.

~

The hardest thing to get used to was the way that Bruno hugged.

Like he was pulling you closer and pushing you away, all at the same time. Great, had been my first reaction: he takes after his father.

But, of course, unlike his father, Bruno can't help it. That third arm's just there, smack dab in the middle of his chest. It's connected to his heart, and some kind of major vein or something. That's why they can't remove it entirely. It's like Bruno's holding his own heart, holding it out to the world.

They offered to chop it off at the shoulder, to amputate. It would look like a big rib, they said, or—at worst—a breast. A breast in the center of his chest.

I thought about it; the doctors insisted I go home and think about it. But all I could think about, no matter how hard I tried to think about the other things, was how from the beginning, that third arm seemed to be connected to Bruno's favorite fingers. How it was a perfectly good arm. How he was a perfectly good little boy.

I said no way.

~

Someday it will be better, I think, as this mother takes her son out of the sandbox and whisks him away, so that it's just me and Bruno again.

Someday, maybe Bruno will even be a ladies' man. The ravishing Ramona will have tried the rest, but then come back to the best—the only boy, she'll say in their wedding toast, who could ever make her squeak.

Bruno looks at me, worried that I'm upset, that he's done something wrong, so I smile at him and make a funny face and tell him his new friend just had to go home.

Then both of us watch as his mother makes a liar out of me and takes her kid to the jungle gym, just across the park, where she is embraced by some of the other mothers, and where the other kids hang on the monkey bars like silent, solemn monkeys, witness to a kill by the watering hole.

I see something move out of the corner of my eye. At first I think it is Bruno giving the departing newbies the finger. Which

I will privately cheer but, of course, publicly disapprove of, for the sake of his social development.

Or maybe it is for me, I think, that finger. And I will accept it, with my head bowed, having expected it since the day I told them to leave it on.

But it isn't either of those things.

Bruno gives me the thumbs up.

That's right, three.

Al Desetta

— ((((

Young Kid Blackie

I was flat on my back in the weeds. Jason sat on me, my chest crushed under his meaty butt, my arms pinned under his blunt knees, as hard as hammers. I could barely breathe.

"Ha-ha," he sang. I gathered everything I could and tried to buck him off with one big lunge but I didn't budge him an inch. A bad idea. It made him only madder.

"No!" I yelled. "I said no, I won't do it, I won't!"

"Why you little bastard," Jason snarled. He sat his weight harder on me and swatted my face with both hands. The air went out of me.

"You do what I tell you to do! When I tell you to do it!"

"C'mon," I sputtered, "I can't breathe! I can't!"

Then the rumble from far away, gaining on us. Then the ground shaking, churned from within, a sheet of wind whipping the grass, my hair, Jason's. The tracks thudding ka-junk, ka-junk, ka-junk, ka-junk, ka-junk, ka-junk, ka-junk—one boxcar, another boxcar, another boxcar, another, another, as I bent my head back to look, to watch them go past upside down. I saw Jason's dumb stare, his slack mouth. I gathered all my strength and tried once again to buck him off.

No luck.

"Whoa!" Jason laughed above the roar, "buckin' bronco!" He cuffed me in the face again. Then the train was gone, it drew the sound after it, like it was turning the air inside out and dragging it all way down the plain and toward the mountains and down the long and flattened track, until it was very far away. Even then you could still hear it, like a warning that it would be back.

"Get off me, Jason! I'm gonna tell!"

"I'm gonna tell," Jason whined. "I'm gonna tell! I'm gonna tell! Why you little sorry bastard."

But suddenly he went slack and I felt him stare again toward the tracks. Then he scrambled off, all the weight completely gone, I could breathe again, I took in a lung's full, then another. I rolled slowly over on my side, my ribs bursting, groping for a rock. I had to get him back, I had to bash him good. Even if he won, I had to do it. I pried a chunk of brick out of the ground with my fingertips and glanced around for him, still on my side, winded, dazed.

When I rose the ground tilted and swirled, I tried to keep it from throwing me over, I did a stutter-step and kept my balance, it didn't twirl as crazily, then I found Jason behind me. I wobbled toward him, the brick in my hand, but he ignored me. He kept his eyes toward the tracks. I feared a trick. Then I turned to look.

A man was standing about twenty feet away. He looked right through me, then his eyes went back to Jason. He stood there for a while, like he thought he had something to say to us. Something to explain. He had some kind of a sack slung over his shoulder. A cap on his head. An old, ragged sweater. Then he walked past us, head down, toward the road to town.

"Who the hell is that?" Jason said.

Arnold ran over, all out of breath, and tugged my sleeve. He'd been watching the whole thing with Jason. He always watched, but he could never do anything about it. "You all right?"

"Yeah," I said, rubbing my elbows.

"Are you sure?"

"Yeah," I said, "I'm okay."

"You see that guy?" Arnold said.

"Yeah."

"Where'd he come from?"

"The tracks."

I glanced again at Jason. No longer distracted, he picked

up a stick and came toward me. I took off limping down the slope
of the field, where the man was headed. Arnold followed.

We caught up to him and kept about ten feet behind him.
When I looked back Jason was following us, but slowly and at a
distance. Ahead was the road. Tony was there, with Boyd and
Butch. They were straddling their bikes. I saw them spit through
their teeth as they watched us approach.

"Shouldn't we go the other way?" Arnold said, dragging on
my arm. "We never get this close to those guys." I kept going and
he yanked harder.

"Relax," I said, prying his fingers off my wrist. My mouth
was like chalk. "Let them try something now."

The man walked toward them as we followed behind. At
the last second Tony and his buddies broke apart and scattered.
Not a sound from them as we passed by, as quiet as church.

"Why don't you try something now," I cried. "Come on,
try something now."

Arnold grabbed my arm again. "What are you doing?"

The man had gotten ahead of us, down the road. We ran
to catch up, then walked along behind on either side. His wrecked
boots crunched the gravel and none of us said a word. A few of the
younger kids trailed at a distance, but straggled, fell behind,
shouted and threw stones into the brush, peeled off one by one,
and then they were gone. We could see the town in the distance.
The church spire.

"You kids know where can a guy do a few chores around
here for a meal?" the man said. His voice was rough but high-
pitched. He shifted the sack onto his other shoulder.

"Mister, where you from?" Arnold asked.

"Maybe your father needs some stuff done," I said to
Arnold. I stayed with Arnold's family when I wasn't at my aunt's.

It was a long walk to his house. Arnold crossed the cool,
shadowed lawn to look for his father while the man and me stood
in the road. I didn't look at him, but kept my hands in my pockets,
kicked hard at some pebbles, stared at his boots. I picked up a

pretty fair-sized stone and threw it as far down the road as I could. Then another, even farther. The front door slammed and Arnold's father came out and watched us from the porch. Then Mr. Henderson came down the steps and crossed the lawn and stopped short, squinting up at the man.

The stars were starting to come out by the time Mrs. Henderson ordered us to wash up. Faces shining, hair slicked back, hands folded, we waited at the dining room table, listening to the rhythm of the grandfather clock. Arnold's father examined his pocket watch.

"Who is he, dad?" Arnold asked.

Mr. Henderson cleared his throat. "His name is Kid Blackie. He's headed on through. He'll only stay the night in return for the chores."

"Theodore," Mrs. Henderson said quietly.

"He split and stacked an entire cord of wood," Mr. Henderson said. "One night only, then he's headed on through."

We heard him on the stairs. Loud, like he wasn't used to stairs. He was cleaned up, but he wore the same ragged sweater. The scab above his eyebrow was still fresh. He watched us closely as we put napkins in our laps and then he did the same. Kid Blackie heaped his plate higher than we ever dared and I kicked Arnold under the table.

"Mr. Blackie," Arnold's father said, his voice sounding like when he doesn't want us to play down by the tracks, "what made you decide to pass through Pueblo?"

He tried to shift the mouthful into his cheek before he spoke. "I ran out of coal to dig in Utah, sir. And no more fruit to pick."

We listened together to the sounds of our eating.

"Were you traveling a long time?"

Kid Blackie chewed and swallowed.

"I got on the rods just outside Salt Lake and that

sonavabi—excuse me, ma'am, I'm sorry—" He made to tip his cap to Arnold's mother although he wasn't wearing it and I kicked Arnold under the table. "—that train didn't want to stop. Thought it would shake me out from under right onto those f—" Arnold kicked me back. "—I'm sorry, ma'am—those darned tracks. Then, just west of here, I rode upstairs with a couple of stiffs and thought I was all set, but then a railroad dick caught me and I'm outside now, holdin' onto the ladder, and he's up on top of the car above me, swinging that billy like a—" He stopped and held himself, then went on. "—and the thing's movin' too fast for me to jump, but the dick wouldn't stop swinging and I thought he would split my head right open with that damned billy before I finally fell off. Thought I'd never stop rolling down that bank of cinders. That's how I got this here." He chuckled and smiled a funny smile. "Then I caught another southbound freight and here I am."

"I see," Mr. Henderson said.

No one said anything.

"Mr. Blackie's a fighter," Mr. Henderson said, "aren't you, Mr. Blackie? Who are you fighting next?" Kid Blackie wanted the butter and Arnold's father handed it over.

"Sir, whomever shows up." He tore the bread with his teeth and a part of it hung from his mouth as he chomped away. Arnold and me kicked each other at the same time. "Wherever I find 'em. Saloons, joints, jungles, in the ring, you name it. Long as I get paid."

Arnold and me laughed, but his folks didn't.

When the meal was done, the tablecloth on Kid Blackie's side looked like a battlefield. He said he'd go out back to stretch. He glanced up at the stars while Arnold and me leaned on the porch railing. He walked into the yard, stared across the black fields, kicked at a stump, then sat on the steps. Then he stood up again, like he couldn't sit still. Arnold's father came to the door and asked if he wanted coffee. They made us go to bed before he turned in.

I had the top bunk, Arnold had the bottom.

"What's a railroad dick?" Arnold said underneath me. "And what's a billy?"

The crickets rasped slowly and heavily. I heard a coyote.

"Don't you know?" I said. I stared at the ceiling, unable to sleep, and hoped he wouldn't ask me again.

It was not yet fully dawn when I heard him on the stairs. I threw back the covers and climbed down. Didn't make a sound in my bare feet. Arnold was curled in a ball, his pillow pulled over his ears. I found my clothes and tiptoed through the door.

He was in the kitchen. He had on the same ragged white sweater, trunks, and those battered boots. The trunks had been white once, just like the sweater. They were speckled with rusty-looking stains, some small like pinpoints, others large and faded.

"Where are you going?"

"I've got to do roadwork, kid. I run every day, to stay in shape."

"Can I run with you?"

He looked at me. The scab was dry and looked better.

"Fine by me," he finally said.

We walked up the side of the house and hit the street at a steady run. We ran up the center of town. We ran past Tony's and then Jason's, and this time I didn't look away, I looked right at the hard faces of their houses, and I saw things I'd been too afraid to look at closely—leaning chimneys and sheds with holes and a swing dangling sideways by one rope out back—and I hoped they were awake and saw us as we went by, our arms and legs pumping. About a half mile outside town I lost him, and walked all the way back and waited for him to return.

Arnold's mother had breakfast ready. I could see that Arnold was jealous when I came in with Kid Blackie. Mrs. Henderson shook her head and turned her back, when, our plates cleaned, we followed him into the backyard.

Hands deep in his pockets, he stood by the pear tree, staring at the yards that bordered the Henderson's. He stared past us, something on his mind.

His eyebrows were as dark as beetles and met angrily at the bridge of his nose. Cheekbones high like an Indian's, his cheeks and jaw were pitted and scarred. His coal-black hair was glazed and stiff, combed back with his fingers. And the stubble on his cheeks seemed to shift into a darker shade whenever he turned, like the coat of Arnold's old gray cat. When he spit it caught the chicken wire of the coop and hung there, fluttering, before it expanded into a string and fell apart.

The Hendersons said there was no more work, so that night Kid Blackie moved to the woods. I followed him there. I told Arnold to tell my aunt, if she asked, that I was still at his place.

He snapped sticks in two and built a fire. He sat across from me, staring into the blaze between us.

"Why don't you go home, kid," he said. "It's gonna be a little cold tonight."

"I like it here in the woods," I said.

"Suit yourself."

The fire flared and crackled between us.

"You warm enough, kid?" he said. He reached into his sack and pulled out a checkered blanket. He tossed it to me, but I kept it at my feet. I wanted to show him that I could take the cold as good as he could.

"Have you had a lot of fights?"

"Quite a few, kid. Been on the road since I was sixteen. Even been to New York."

"New York," I said. "What happened in New York?"

"Three broken ribs and a $35 purse. That's $10 a rib, plus $2.50 for each black eye. The rest was free. Try riding the rods sometime with three busted ribs."

He lit a cigarette with a stick from the fire.

"John Lester Johnson," he said. "He was 215. Maybe I was 170, soaking wet."

It felt good to be alone, to need no one, to finally be afraid of no one, deep in the woods. He slept against a tree, his sweater spread over his shoulders. I watched the coals glow and crackle a long time before I fell asleep.

In the morning, when I awoke, the checkered blanket was draped over me. He was crouched by the fire. He yanked a couple of potatoes from the coals and tossed me one. The outside was charred, but the inside was fluffy and warm. We ate them. Then we ran. Along the road, past the fields. Kids stopped to watch us. He lost me after a half-mile or so, and I waited for him back in the woods. When he came back it was almost noon. He sat across from me, the dead fire between us, his sweater strung around his neck like a towel.

"Kid, those two spuds were my last. We're gonna have to hustle."

He reached in his sack. He pulled out a toy monkey on strings. With his fingers working, he made it dance.

"See this here? I carry him everywhere. My gloves, my ring shoes, my trunks, and him. We're going into the saloon in town. They have a free lunch table. The thing is, you have to buy a beer to go to the lunch table. And I don't have a nickel to buy a beer. You wait outside the saloon while I go in. After about five minutes, you come inside. I'll be sitting next to someone. You go on the other side of who that is, and entertain him with this."

He shook the monkey.

"And keep him entertained. Understand?"

I waited outside Mickey's. I heard laughter inside, music. When I walked in I couldn't see, because my eyes weren't adjusted. Then I saw Mr. Harris at the bar. Mr. Harris was always at the bar. Kid Blackie was on the stool to his right.

I walked up to Mr. Harris, to his left side, and jiggled the monkey.

"What the blazes is that," Mr. Harris said. His arms were folded on the bar. He had a beer in front of him, about half full.

"I can make him talk," I said. "Watch."

I jiggled the monkey and made it talk, and Mr. Harris turned sideways and kept his watery eyes on me. On his other side I saw Kid Blackie checking to make sure the bartender wasn't looking. Then, real slow and easy, he took Mr. Harris's beer and slid quietly off his stool and ambled toward the lunch table.

Now I tried to make the monkey sing. Mr. Harris smiled.

"Where the devil did you get that piece of shit?" he said.

Back in the woods, Kid Blackie unloaded his pockets. Hardboiled eggs. Pickles. Squashed sandwiches.

"For a nickel beer you can put away a lot of food," he said. "Especially when your hands are fast."

The next day we did the monkey thing in the bar. The third day the bartender caught on.

"Busted again," Kid Blackie said. He picked at his teeth, propped lazily against a log by the fire. "I need a stiff to roll."

He saw that I didn't understand.

"Or maybe there's some two-bit pest around that no one wants. Someone people will pass the hat for me to flatten. You know anyone?"

"Jason Crumly," I said.

"Oh yeah?" He turned his broken face to me, chewing gum steadily. "Who's this Jason?"

My stomach surged like it does each July 4th, at the first sight of fireworks high in the sky.

"Usually down by the tracks," I said. "He should be there now."

"That field by the tracks?" Kid Blackie said. "This Jason's a railroad dick?"

"He's this kid who always picks on me. Every day he starts something."

"Picks on you? A kid?"

He seemed disgusted as he looked past me.

"Yeah, but he's a big kid," I said. "And I'll pay you. Four bits."

I stood up and pulled my pocket inside out, took out the gum, the rubber ball, the chocolate encrusted with lint, and gave him a glimpse of the coins. Kid Blackie stared, chewing steadily.

"Where'd you get four bits?"

"I saved it up," I said. "He's a bully. Him and his friends. He picks on everyone who's smaller."

"There must be some pest in that bar," he said.

He tossed pebbles into the fire circle. It was like we were trying to outwait each other.

"Jesus Christ," he finally said. "Four stinking bits."

He walked behind me on the way to the field, his boots crunching the gravel. Kids called out when they saw us, caught up, trailed after at a distance.

Jason was in the field with the others. They were hurling rocks at a freight parked on a siding.

"That him?" Kid Blackie asked.

"The big one, the one with the cap."

"Damn," he muttered. He held out his fingers. I gave him the money.

Tony and Boyd and Butch didn't move until Blackie was right on top of them, then they trotted down the slope alongside their bikes and jumped into the saddles and coasted down the field, staring back over their shoulders as they rode. But Jason didn't run. Blackie stopped in front of him, his hands in his pockets, and from where I stood in the road he looked like he was talking to Jason. He laughed, and then Jason laughed, and Kid Blackie looked at the ground, laughing, and then both of them were looking at the ground. Then Kid Blackie put up his fists and shook them like he wanted Jason to take a swing at him. Jason took an easy swing and Kid Blackie blocked it just as easy. Then Kid Blackie set his feet again, and Jason took another playful swing and Kid Blackie landed an easy swing back. Then Kid Blackie raised his fists again and motioned to Jason, and Jason swung a little harder and Kid Blackie lashed out and Jason was down on his knees, then down on his face completely, his hands under his stomach as he twisted and tried to kick his feet, and then he turned slowly on his side and just laid there. Blackie stood over him, fists clenched. He glanced back at me, then around the field. He stepped over Jason and climbed the long slope to the road.

"Sonavabitch swung on me," he said quickly as we walked along.

I slapped him on his shoulder and he was hard like a horse. He wheeled around and flung my hand away. Then he moved toward me and I darted back. When he stopped I just stood in the road, watching him. Then after a while he started walking again and I followed after.

"How did you become a fighter?"

He didn't answer me at first. At times he looked more Indian than others.

"My brother, he was a fighter. He had me punching a bag when I was younger than you. One of those homemade things, filled with sawdust, in the shed out back."

"Was your brother a good fighter?"

"Glass chin," he said. "Could dish it out but couldn't take it." His eyes went dead for a moment and he shook his head. "Bernie," he said.

I tossed a stick on the fire.

"Kid, you got a home to go to? Where are your folks?"

"I ran way from my folks. I live with my aunt now."

"Ran away? Why?"

I didn't say anything more. I kept my eyes on the fire. I waited for him to ask me again, but he didn't.

"Ran away," he repeated, like he was talking to himself. "Well, I guess that makes the two of us."

Mr. Schmidt nodded to the bucket behind the counter.

"There it is. What the hell do you want beef brine for?"

I didn't answer him. I lifted the bucket. I had to take short stutter steps to not slosh any on the floor. Mr. Schmidt watched me from the counter to make sure I didn't. Somehow I got the screen door open without spilling any.

I carried it down the dusty main street of town. I had to shift hands often. It was the color of plums, with tiny islands of honey-colored fat on its shifting surface. I stared at them, as they bunched and separated, jiggling with the rhythm of my walking. I sloshed the pail every now and then, and the brine raised a puff of dust before it darkened the earth.

When I reached the woods, Kid Blackie set the pail before him.

"Good job," he said.

He took out a handkerchief, soaked it in the pail, and then rubbed in into his forehead as he leaned back. Dipped it again, and rubbed it over his cheeks, eyes, nose. His face looked bronze. I tried to wave the stench away.

"Stinks to holy hell," Kid Blackie said. "Bernie had me doing this since I was 12. Toughens your skin like leather, so they can't stop a fight on cuts. Want some, kid?"

He squeezed the rag, the brine seeping from his fist like dirty rain.

At noon, the sun high, we played cards on a stump by the tracks, as the little kids gathered to stare. When we stood up, they moved away. I walked at Kid Blackie's side, my face grim and hard. Arnold tried to talk to me as we crossed the field, but I ignored him and pushed past. I didn't need him anymore.

Kid Blackie stopped in the road to pick up a rock as the old gray cat crossed in front of us. I looked for a stick, but before I could find one I heard a sharp yowl and the cat bounded heavily into the brush. Tony and Butch and Boyd watched from the field. Jason wasn't there; no one had seen him for a couple of days.

One night we huddled before the blaze in the deep part of the woods. The moon was hidden and it was very dark. Kid Blackie lit a cigarette. He dragged on it and the coal for an instant revealed his face.

"I got a fight, kid," he said. "Got a wire in town today. In Ely, over in Nevada."

He spit into the fire. His arms were crossed, the sweater draped over them, over his wide shoulders.

"Is he good?" I asked.

"It's a decent fight, kid," Blackie said. "It'll give me a nice stake. A couple of hundred in it for me, easy. I win, and no more riding the rods for a while."

I heard a coyote far across the plain, long and drawn out. I couldn't tell if it was one coyote and an echo, or several sounding one after the other, close together.

Blackie yawned, flicked his cigarette into the brush. "I need a decent meal, kid, something not pickled, not out of a can. I can't go into the ring a scarecrow."

The fire fell into embers and the crickets rose around us.

"They got lots of food at that friend of yours."

"The Henderson's?" I said.

Arnold's window opened after I dinged it with a third pebble. He met me in the backyard. The moon was out now and he seemed a gray shadow as he approached me. He was in pajamas. I grabbed him by the collar.

"What's going on?" Arnold stammered, eyes wide as he stumbled back. "What are you doing?" I grabbed him again, pulled him close to my face.

"Don't say a word. Kid Blackie needs something to eat."

"Where am I going to get it?"

I pushed him toward the back door. Even in the kitchen we could hear Mr. Henderson snore. The steady, muffled rattle was our signal. Whenever it stopped, we stopped. Whenever it sounded, Arnold filled a bag with everything it could hold— turkey, ham, cheese, rolls, bread, fruit. I told him to hurry.

Kid Blackie stood in the shadow alongside the icebox. There wasn't much moonlight in the kitchen, but I saw him motion to me. When I came up close, Mr. Henderson's snoring and Kid Blackie's whisper mixed together.

"What room's his old man in?" Kid Blackie said.

I couldn't see his face. Everything had gone to black, except the glint in his eyes under those hard brows—that was all I saw.

"I said, what room's his old man in?" he said again.

I tried to say something. I heard a voice in the parlor and I froze.

I listened for a while, then I stepped to the doorway and peered around the corner.

"Who's that?" Mr. Henderson said from the top of the stairs.

The light of a lantern jerked along the wall and the steps creaked. The lantern caught Blackie's face and threw his shadow crazily against the kitchen floor.

"Kid Blackie," Mr. Henderson said, "is that you?"

Kid Blackie said nothing.

"I wasn't sure who was there."

Then I heard Mrs. Henderson from behind her door at the top of the stairs: "Theodore, is everything all right?"

"We were just getting some food, Mr. Henderson," I said. "We were a little low." He raised the lantern higher and looked at me.

"Oh, sure, Mr. Blackie," Mr. Henderson said quietly, ignoring me. He was now halfway down the stairs. "I suspect you're a little short until your next fight. Take what you need." He turned to the upstairs bedroom. "You go back to bed, honey. There's no problem. It's only Kid Blackie."

We followed the road under the moon's lopsided egg until we reached the woods. We fought our way blindly through the underbrush and brambles.

No one came near to me or to Kid Blackie anymore. No kids trailed after us. As we walked through the field each morning, Tony and the rest would scatter aside on their bikes, to let us pass at a safe distance.

"We haven't forgotten Jason," Tony called after, just loud enough for me to hear. "Stick tight to your bodyguard, while you have him."

I'd keep up with Kid Blackie each dawn for as long as I could, and then watch him loping off toward the mountains as I slowed to a breathless walk. I watched him until there was only the road and the mountains.

Late one afternoon I found him in the deep part of the woods, crouched down low over the dead fire.

"Should we try the bar again?" I said.

He was crouched with his back to me. He traced a stick through the cold embers. He pulled a blackened tin can from the coals, flung it behind him into the brush. He snapped off sapling branches and covered the ashes with green leaves. He rose and lifted his sack.

"I've got that fight, kid," he said. "There's a freight coming through."

I followed him through the woods. I kept my eyes on the ground but I still tripped once or twice. Branches whipped my face. When we reached the road, he turned to face me.

He ruffled my hair with his giant hand, then he pulled me by the neck and held me against him for a moment. Then he pushed me gently away, threw the sack on his shoulder, and started down the field toward the tracks.

I wanted to say something to him. I wanted to follow him but I couldn't move. "Kid," I said, my voice weak and useless, just before he disappeared down the slope.

I walked along the road, headed toward town. I heard the gravel crunching quickly behind me and turned. Arnold walked swiftly past on the far side of the road. It was dinner time and that was where he was headed. He took the same route, at the same time, every day. I lifted my hand from habit and started to say something, but he scooted ahead of me and didn't slow down for a moment, even as he glanced back.

The road went along the field. I looked toward the tracks. Jason was there, and Tony, and all the rest of them. They were about halfway down the field, straddling their bikes. I saw them spit through their teeth. Then they looked up and saw me. I felt like running, but I didn't. I picked up a good-sized rock and I threw it as far down the road as I could.

Scott Maxwell

———————————————————————————— ❨❨

Guessing

Sad music is pouring out of my neighbor's little house as twilight sets in. I'm on the porch with a lit cigarette and an ice cold dark beer, watching her windows like I'm expecting them to all of a sudden blow to pieces. Her boyfriend came back from Florida married to a size three woman; she told me this halfway through her second liter of red wine. The music is like a medicine I assume; she cranks up the volume to slightly beneath absolute annoyance and sways away. I don't know what she does or what she feels. I'm only left to my guesses.

Roaring down I-87 this afternoon, I saw a construction worker standing atop an overpass, leaning against the railing. It was odd for there was no construction taking place; there were no other workers around him, nor any machinery. I wondered what he was doing there. I thought about my friend Ian telling me that if he were going to kill himself he'd hang himself on an overpass during rush hour traffic. I remember looking at the cars flowing below me as I walked over an overpass one day. I stopped in the center and placed my hands on the railing and looked to see if there was a place to tie a rope.

I zoomed past the construction worker and looked into the rearview mirror, catching a glimpse of his orange jacket and hard-hat. I wondered if the other drivers that sped past him were also wondering why he stood all alone. I wondered if the construction worker is still on their brains like he is on mine. I assumed some people wondered, but quickly left their wonderment, slipping back into the esoteric realm of their own lives, asking themselves questions like: "What am I cooking for dinner?" "Did Shaun remember to pay his car insurance or am I going to have to do it again?" A construction worker standing alone on an interstate overpass is not something easily remembered, but if he died on that interstate people would struggle to forget.

I played a possible scenario over in my head as I continued driving south on I-87. I imagined the construction worker standing upright from his lean. I imagined him looking out into the sea of cars flowing past him, hearing each one coming closer, the sounds of the engines reaching their climax right under him and then making the same sounds backwards as they drove away. I imagined him refraining from blinking as he stepped out, off the overpass, into traffic.

A car hit him at seventy miles per hour and projected his body several feet onto the concrete. The driver who hit him didn't realize her heart could pump so rapidly and still stay inside her chest. Numerous people saw this occur. He was dead instantly. His soul left his body like a rocket ship, never expected to return. People rushed out of their cars to what was left of his body. Maybe his head was broken open like a watermelon, leaking onto the roadway, or an arm or a leg came off, looking like shredded pork at the end that was once attached to his body. I just don't know what happens to our bodies when they are hit with seventy-mile-an-hour steel and glass, so I guess.

In minutes people will meet a traffic jam and bang on the steering wheel with open palms; they'll curse for they're already late to pick up their kid from soccer practice or spend an evening with their lawyer, and they'll curse in a tone that means things like this aren't supposed to happen to them; this is a situation they're supposed to read about in a newspaper article while waiting for a train. Kids will get yelled at by their parents for complaining that their seatbelts are making them nauseous. Couples will argue. Truckers will talk to one another via CB radio with such seriousness one would think they just called in an air raid on South Vietnam. Several cell phones will be seen from car windows perched on ears like wall smoke detectors. Maybe some guy will call his wife and say, "Honey I'm caught in traffic, it's like a standstill, just my luck ya know, I'm sorry." Possibly his wife will think he's lying, maybe he cheated on her in the past. Maybe she calls the New York State Thruway Authority to confirm that there is in fact a hold up. Maybe later on in the evening her paranoia will make her display so much guilt that her husband asks her what's wrong and she can't tell him and he jumps to conclusions.

There will be red lights flashing and sirens of course. "Stay back" and "Move along" will be expressions used to redundancy. The officers who are forced to repeat them will be hearing them in their sleep; possibly they will wake up in a cold sweat having dreamt that they didn't say them clearly enough and they were at fault for another accident; maybe it was a small child and people will give them funny looks at the hardware store or overcook their eggs at the diner they frequent.

The fact of the matter will remain simple. "A man died tonight after being hit by a Ford Taurus traveling on Interstate Eighty-even outside of Coxsackie, New York. Our sources tell us that authorities on site are not giving out the name of the man, but we know he was pronounced dead on arrival after he jumped or fell from an overpass into traffic and was struck by a car. The man was possibly a construction worker of some kind, yet no one is sure why he was up on the overpass at all. Further details will be presented as quickly as they come to us."

People will see a break in traffic and hit their foot on the accelerator, saying "All right, we're finally outta here!" Yet when they see the holdup is not caused by construction they will take their foot off the accelerator and creep their cars past the accident scene trying to memorize each detail like the photographic memory of a grandmaster tries to memorize a chess board. A paralyzing calm will take over their bodies while they view the tragedy. The passers-by will take it all in. Everyone will want to know what has happened. It will be as if the stress of impatience left their ligaments so quickly it never existed at all. Maybe they'll see a body bag, maybe they'll see blood smeared all over the concrete with chunks of skin and bone or his leg mangled and disfigured, being carried by an EMT. Maybe they will only see the medics and the flashing lights and will leave uninformed and disappointed.

I bet that everyone who can't figure out what has happened turns on their TV when they get home, for their curiosity will be too much to withstand. I bet when someone brings up the accident at work in the ensuing days people will rush to say, "I was right there when it happened!" I bet they will make things up that didn't occur, only to sound more informed, more involved.

Everyone that was present will remember the construction worker who killed himself by stepping into traffic on I-87 in the summer of 2002. Everyone will think of the previous impossibility of a construction worker committing suicide in such a horrific manner and silently everyone will watch for it to happen again, so as not to miss one single detail that they mistakenly missed before.

In twenty years a grandfather will show his grandchildren the spot where the construction worker was struck and the kids will ask a very obvious question, but a question not pondered at the immediate time of the accident: "Why did he do it, Grandpa?" The question will hit a chord that the grandfather has thought about several times over and he will once again wonder briefly to himself why someone would take their own life. The grandfather will emit a dissatisfied sigh and reply the safest way possible, saying "I guess he just didn't want to live anymore." Why will it be so difficult to remember the construction worker alive, just standing, arms folded, looking and breathing?

The music has turned off at her house as the darkness has draped over the sun. The construction worker is somewhere I'll never know, not thinking about me and not knowing I'm thinking about him. Carol, I imagine, is getting ready for bed, possibly humming the last sad song she didn't let end. She's getting ready for the next day like all of us, suffering with the Armageddon in her head, succeeding in composing herself to make it less obvious.

I take a sip of my dark beer that has nestled itself into the matching backdrop of the night. I put the cigarette butt out on the sole of my shoe, for I keep forgetting to bring out the ashtray. I snicker. One would think by this time I'd have remembered to grab it. I let out a sigh and crack my neck. The fireflies are twinkling like stars and the crickets are singing once again, as reliable as inconveniences, as predictable as you and I.

Holly Beye

The Dolls' House

Haskell sits in the red plush armchair, straight up, the remote control held loosely in his thin hand. Someone has put a thick gray shawl—100 per cent wool—around his shoulders. Perhaps he himself did it earlier this afternoon when he came to the parlor to sit by the wood stove and watch television. The television is on, but he's been too preoccupied to take it in. Every once in a while he jerks to attention and scans his way through all the channels, proof to anyone entering the sitting room that at 65 he is still very much in control of his faculties.

It is Sunday, the 22nd of January. Outside, the landscape glitters grayly. There has been no snow since the first week of December. It is cold, five below zero.

"She said she would call," keeps running through his mind. He is not sure whether he said this in response to an actual event or as part of the dialogue in a dream.

He feels he should talk to someone about this, knowing all the same there is no one left in his life with whom he can share this matter. His thin, white face is hairless. Even his eyelashes have thinned out so that the tears that have been inexplicably welling up all afternoon roll unchecked down his cheeks, leaving the rims around his eyes raw and red.

In the distance, the hall phone rings. It is answered on the third count. Since one o'clock this afternoon, the phone has rung 11 times. Never once was it for him.

None of the other nine boarders comes near him in age. Four of them are not yet 30, and two of these are still in college.

Of the other five, none is over 55. Wage earners. No one is even thinking about retiring.

Mrs.Keough, the landlady, is 59. Arthritis has swollen her knees and ankles to twice their normal size. She walks like a crab, supporting herself with two canes. She is in pain a good deal of the time. Yet even Mrs.Keough, a widow with children living far away, does not think of retirement.

The heavy sliding door is rolled back abruptly and a girl of 20 with long, bushy, straw-colored hair glides in, carrying a large book and an apple out of which a bite has been taken.

"Mr. Carmody, I'm going to study here next to the stove, OK?" she says in a soft, sullen voice, pushing in the button on the TV and plopping herself into the wide brown leatherette chair opposite Haskell. She has brought with her into the room a lovely fragrance.

"It's pretty dark over there," he says as she opens her heavy book and squints at the pages, turning them slowly, abstractedly, all the while taking aggressive chunks out of the apple. "Don't you want a light?"

"I know it's dark!" she snaps back, tossing the apple core into the stove where it sizzles and fills the room with burnt apple smell. "I'm only trying to memorize some lines!"

Tears push to the edges of his eyes. He turns away from her, trying to imagine a dialogue they could be having. But his daydream is interrupted by the ringing of the hall phone once again.

The girl leaps from her chair, the heavy book falling to the floor face down, a good handful of its pages cruelly crushed. "I'll get it! I'll get it!" she screams, not bothering to pull the sliding door shut behind her.

The exquisite fragrance remains. He is overwhelmed by the memory of Chopin's *Polonaise*... an open window... the soft April wind following on the heels of an afternoon shower catching at the lavender muslin curtains... the house next door... and Clara Wallace, inside, standing on tiptoe and cupping her mouth in her hands, pokes her head out to call to him: "Haskell! Haskell! Come on over! I'm going to play with the dolls' house now...!"

He sees himself, a thin, long-necked boy of 10, in gray wool knee socks and visor cap, hastening across the 30-foot lawn separating their two wide, three-storied houses, to join the handful of neighborhood children clambering up the back staircase to the Wallaces' third floor playroom.

Clara Wallace's doll house was two stories high, set on a wooden platform. The family handyman had been commissioned to make it for her in time for Christmas last year when she had just turned nine. The dolls were china and came from Germany. You could buy them in Woolworth's for 10 cents. They had movable arms and legs and when the wires for these wore out, Clara would replace them with pins. A couple of Clara's dolls were now held together with a second set of pins at both the arms and the legs.

One of them—Peter Pan—had, in addition to pins, a large bandage resembling a turban around his head, which had been stepped on once during a fight between Clara and one of her brothers. A less caring person would more than likely have thrown out the six-inch 10-cent doll with a crushed skull, but Clara Wallace had pushed and pulled the back of his head into place with her stubby, fat fingers and corseted it in a massive headdress. From then on, Clara had assigned Peter the starring role in each one of the original dramas performed under her direction by her five dolls.

Haskell had suspected that blond Wendy, who had real hair, not painted on like the others, must be very jealous of Peter's ascendancy. *I'd be*, he told himself. Even now, as he remembers those extraordinary adventures when Peter, always at the very last minute, the situation for each and every one of the others utterly doomed, came to the rescue; even today, Haskell remembers the overwhelming jealousy he'd felt. On Wendy's behalf. She was so plump and earthy and useless, not having any special powers in that matted yellow wig. But before Peter's accident, she'd been the star.

The doll house adventures had ended abruptly one day when Clara and he were 12. She had just said bluntly that she wouldn't be doing it any more. He couldn't understand it, was depressed for days afterwards, went moping around with his hands in his pockets at a loss for anything to do. Twenty years later, pondering her behavior together with his therapist, Haskell had thought her decision might have coincided with her getting her first brassiere.

The girl is back in the parlor room once again. She slams the door shut, lifts her foot and violently kicks the book she has left lying on the floor. His instinct tells him it is Shakespeare, not Ibsen or Chekhov. He knows a thing or two about textbooks for community college courses in drama. He has spent 30 years in the teaching profession. This book fetches a good price, the volume is over-size, printed in double columns, on 16-pound paper, and has footnotes in boldface type at the bottom of every page. She should not have kicked it.

"You shouldn't kick a book," Haskell says, surprising himself since he has vowed never to speak to her again following her earlier rudeness about the light. He looks up, wincing in unconscious anticipation of a cruel remark or possibly a shoe flung in his direction.

"Fuck you," she murmurs without emphasis. The last rays of the afternoon sun have formed a shimmering path from the window high up behind her to the faded Oriental rug on which she stands. As she turns away from Haskell's glance, two tears rolling down her cheeks catch the sun's rays and sparkle like crystals.

She realizes Haskell has seen her tears. "I can't help it," she cries softly, throwing herself into the big leather chair and putting her face in her hands.

How he would like to help her! He sees himself rising from his chair, walking over to her side, and bending down to stroke her hair very gently. He might even call her Wendy, explaining about the doll and its uncombable hair so like her own.... Would she like a glass of water? But her body is racked with sobs now. Curled up in a tight little ball in the big armchair, she has turned her back on him.

Now that she is crying, he's shut down entirely. He used to be a great crier himself, but was never public about it. When he was a boy, he would lie on his bed upstairs, his fist stuffed in his mouth, or the pillow over his head, so that no one would hear him. Not that anyone was likely to. It was a big house. He was an only child. His parents spent their evenings downstairs in separate rooms—his mother in the large, brightly lighted living room, compulsively knitting little garments for grandchildren Haskell might present her with when he grew up, Daddy Carmody in the den reading the memoirs of military patriots as soon as they were published. The only time his parents talked was when Daddy Carmody would go out to the kitchen to mix up refills for their martinis, for which he was rightly famous.

After Daddy Carmody died, his mother's highest accolade when honoring his memory was always "He made a mean martini."

"He made a hell of a martini," says Haskell out loud, and immediately looks to the girl, ready to deny what he has, very much in spite of himself, just said. But she is still too deeply buried in her own grief to care one whit about his.

"I just said something I didn't expect to—" He pauses. "I've been waiting for a call, too," he finally says, realizing that her utter indifference to his presence is giving him license to say aloud whatever comes to his mind. "All day...." He pauses.

Again he is overwhelmed by the girl's fragrance, which her emotional outburst has reactivated. Spring flowers... clover... violets, in particular.... He would sit at the open window practicing his piano lesson after school. It was the only thing at which he excelled—practicing the piano. He knew that upstairs in the playroom where she sat in front of her doll house, Clara was listening to his playing. The year his teacher had given him Chopin's *Etude* to study was the year Wendy went into her decline and he liked to think his music was helping Wendy in her grief over being superseded by Peter.

Even now, it is excruciatingly painful to think about. How Clara laughed at him when he asked her to give him the doll after she'd stopped playing with the dolls' house.

"What d'you want her for, she's only a doll!" But in the searching, sneering look Clara had given him was a streak of black despair.

With the onset of puberty, they'd gone their separate ways. Growing pudgier, Clara had gone all out for clubs and good grades. Haskell collected comic books and took over his father's job as his mother's bartender, liberally medicating himself from her bountiful supply. By the time he graduated from high school he had formed a dependency relationship with alcohol that allowed him to function competently but without distinction as long as he remained under-employed.

"I never married." He goes on talking over the girl's muffled weeping in the background. "I've retired because I couldn't think what else to do. My voice has no resonance. I live here because I'm afraid of being alone... I do not drink before five in the afternoon...."

She has stopped crying and is gaping at him. He gets up crookedly out of his chair and shuffles over to her.

"At least you got a phone call!" he hisses as he bends over her, hands on his hips, swaying dangerously. "You got a phone call!" Shouting.

It has come to him as a sudden dark warning that the fragrance she wears which put him in such vivid contact with those memories of over 50 years ago has gotten sour through mixing with the fear and sadness of her glands. If he stays with her a moment longer, her presence will have the power to turn those memories into something fierce and trivial and dull.

The girl leaps from her chair screaming, "Get away from me you dirty old man! You dirty old—!" throwing her thin body violently against his so that he falls face down on the floor, where he remains until well after the dinner hour.

Barbara Brooks

)) ————————————————————————

Girls and Women Half-Naked

On the last Saturday afternoon of summer, Jerry drove to Manhattan from thirty miles north of the city, then crossed from the East Side to the West Side, picking up his daughter's friends. At each girl's brownstone or high-rise he double-parked and got out of his Range Rover to ring a buzzer and shake a parent's hand, to make room for another sleeping bag, pillow, backpack, unruly head of hair hanging loose or knotted, camp-tanned legs and arms, skinny ankles and wrists tied with colored threads and beads. Each girl wore boxer shorts rolled to the crest of her budding hips and a skimpy t-shirt, exposing a flat belly. Jerry's new wife Nora, eight months pregnant with her first child, reclined beside him in the passenger seat. She had come along for the ride as proof to the parents that a woman would help chaperone the party.

In the over-stuffed car, there were five girls so far—two Mollies, a Kelly, a Dana and a Brynn; due to a complicated matrix of timing and geography, Jerry would pick up his own daughter last. He hated getting Lucy in the city, because it reminded him that she had another home: another closet full of clothes, other pets and another lime green iMac with bootleg copies of the software he had bought and paid for. Two or three times a week he drove into the city to pick her up, and he often fantasized starting some kind of pseudo-charitable recycling service, in which kids who had nothing could use the duplicate possessions that belonged to kids who had two homes.

Jerry double-parked in front of Lucy's building and rang the buzzer. She had been at camp in Vermont for eight weeks, the longest she'd ever been away, and now his heart raced like a schoolboy's as he waited to see her again.

"Daddy!" she called from a second-floor window. "Up here." Jerry looked up and saw a blur of curly, dark hair. "Mom wants to talk to you."

Before he could answer, Lucy pulled her head back inside.

Nora struggled to sit up in the passenger seat, which she had cranked back to nearly flat.

"Liz is coming down?" Nora asked. Her cheeks were flushed, and her short blonde bangs were damp against her forehead. Since becoming pregnant, she was overheated all the time.

"Sit tight, love," Jerry said, coming back to the car. He kissed Nora through the window. "This'll be quick."

As Lucy and her mother approached, Jerry was caught off-guard by how much they looked alike. He saw that over the summer, Lucy had begun developing breasts, and her legs had grown longer. Now her shape was unmistakably Liz's: wide-hipped yet relatively flat from front to back, like a guitar. They had the same hair.

"My god," Jerry said out loud, more to himself than to Liz or Nora. "Look how she's changed." Until now, he had always thought Lucy looked more like him.

Nora sat up in her seat and whistled. "She looks amazing."

"Hey, hon," Jerry called to Lucy. He bent down to kiss her, but she pushed past him on her way to her friends in the car.

"Just let her go," Liz said. "It's a whole new ballgame now."

Lucy smacked on the car until one of the girls unlocked the back door for her. Nora got out of the front seat and stretched her arms over her head. In her skimpy tie-dyed tank top and colorful cotton skirt, she looked like a pregnant hippie who loved not only her own body but everybody else's also.

Jerry watched the two women check each other out. If he took his sweet time that way, looking at a woman's eyes and hair, shoulders, breasts and hips, they'd write him off as an asshole dinosaur. Both women were tanned from the sun and wore a sparkly gold lipstick he had never noticed on either of them before. Liz wore a white undershirt and old jeans patched with pieces of a red bandana. Like Nora, she never wore a bra.

Liz put her palm on Nora's stomach. "Ooh," she said. "I love a pregnant belly. Long as it's not mine." Then she hugged Nora for what seemed to Jerry to be a very long time. "Just kidding. You look beautiful."

"You think?" Nora said. She ran her hands over her stomach. "Jerry thinks I'll get way bigger."

"Yeah, well," Liz said. "That's Jerry. He always needs a little more time." She winked at Nora.

"She's got another three weeks," Jerry said, pulling Nora closer toward him. "That could mean a month." He still had a banister to build for their stairs and another coat of blue paint to do in the baby's room. Lucy had come early, but that couldn't possibly mean anything now.

"I bet he's still got stuff to do in the house," Liz said.

"Yup," Nora said. "And I know I'm going to be early."

Suddenly the radio blasted on, and the car began to rock as girls climbed between the back seat and the front. Lucy opened the sunroof and began to climb through it.

"Get back in there!" Liz shook her fist at Lucy in a mock gesture of discipline. "She's so wound up, you'll barely know her."

"Liz," Jerry said, "what's up? We've got to get on the road."

She told him that over the summer she had become certified as a massage therapist. "We need to look at our schedule."

"Really?" Jerry said. He never considered paying for a massage, but he knew plenty of people who did. His boss, Andrew, for one; he paid eighty dollars every week for a masseuse to come to his home. Maybe Jerry could hook Andrew up with Liz.

"People like to get massages in the evening," Liz said. "So I'll need you to take Lucy another night." She always asked him for things in front of other people, or on the fly.

"We'll have to talk about it later," Jerry said. In the twenty years he'd known Liz, she'd changed jobs dozens of times, and he always had to help her somehow.

"Why later?"

"I don't know," Jerry said. "With the baby, we have to see."

"It'll be okay," Nora said. "I'll be home at night." Jerry was surprised, annoyed, to hear her offer.

"Nora," Jerry said. "Let me worry about this with Liz."

"What difference does it make?" Nora said brushing her hand in the air. "My life won't be my own for a long time." Then she turned to Liz. "Can I come up and use the bathroom?"

"Sure, sweetie," Liz said.

As they went inside Jerry wondered when Nora and Liz had become so friendly. Initially, they had met only over pick-ups and drop-offs; then last spring before Lucy left for camp, the women had begun to make the plans. Now he remembered that one summer night, while Lucy was away, Jerry had followed Nora's voice into the kitchen where he found her with her feet up and a mug of tea in her hand. From her breezy tone, he thought she was on the phone with a friend, or her sister. She'd cut the conversation short when she heard him come into the room.

"You never told me Liz was so funny," Nora had said some time after putting down the phone. This caught Jerry by surprise, but he hadn't asked Nora what she meant. Later, he thought about asking her if Liz had been the one on the other end of the phone, but it seemed too far-fetched.

Now, waiting for Nora in the car, Jerry was confused. His daughter looked more like his ex-wife than a child. His new wife was friends with his old wife, and they were upstairs without him and the curtains were drawn. Overcome by the smell of an open bottle of nail polish, Jerry rolled down his window and, without turning around, said, "Hey, don't spill that," to no one in particular. He wished he could have some time alone with Lucy—to sit and talk and laugh like they used to—but he knew he'd have to wait until tomorrow, until the other girls went home, or until it was Lucy's idea. Jerry closed his eyes and let the high-pitched voices wash over him, until Nora eventually opened the door.

Jerry knew every bend in the road toward home, and with Nora asleep and most of the girls singing and shrieking and passing headphones and CD players around, he did a mental inventory of the paraphernalia he had rented and assembled in the yard: two three-man tents, six lanterns, and twice as many Citronella torches as he should need. He knew how much Lucy hated bugs. He had hidden party favors in the bushes and the trees, and drawn and photocopied a treasure map and a list of clues.

Jerry remembered how flattered he had been when Lucy called from camp to say she wanted to have her thirteenth birthday party not at a skating rink or clay art studio, but rather in tents pitched in his backyard.

"Aren't you tired yet of camping?" he had asked, assuming she'd spent much of the summer outside. He had missed visiting day because of a business trip, so he didn't know much about her summer.

"A little," she said, "but most of my school friends didn't go to camp this year. They'll think it's cool."

In the five years since Jerry moved out of the city, Lucy had brought only a few of her friends to visit. Now, Jerry was grateful for his big back yard. He could make hot dogs and s'mores for the girls. He'd supply flashlights and a short-wave radio. He imagined telling ghost stories in the dark. He told Lucy he could plan a scavenger hunt.

"Easy, Daddy," she'd told him on the phone. "Just get tents." Jerry hadn't listened.

When they were halfway home, Nora woke up. The way she rubbed her eyes and her face, and yawned out loud, Jerry thought of a mother lion, disoriented and starved after a long hibernation. "Feed me," her eyes seemed to say.

Nora looked back at the girls. They all had headphones on and were yelling at each other over their music, but she cupped her hand over the side of her mouth and spoke softly to Jerry. "She seems content," she said.

"How can you tell?" Jerry said, looking in the rear view mirror. "She hasn't said three words to me."

"Who hasn't?"

"Lucy."

"I meant Liz," Nora said. "The massage thing seems good."

"Please," Jerry said. "I've been here a hundred times."

Jerry wanted to say Liz was and always had been completely irresponsible, and that this job would last no longer than any of the others, but he was afraid Lucy might overhear.

"Is that fair?" Nora asked, as though she read his mind.

"Here we go." Jerry accused Nora of always siding with the woman, regardless of the evidence or the crime. "She's keeping to the pattern," Jerry said. "Leave it at that."

Jerry knew Nora had heard him tell his friends that after exhausting all the sit-down jobs in the city, Liz was now working her way through the ones she could do standing up. So far, she'd passed out perfume samples at a Japanese makeup store, swapped numbered tickets for people's smelly shoes at the last bowling alley in Manhattan, and made six-dollar vegetable juices, which she sold from a cart in Washington Square Park. Thanks to Jerry's child support, she'd been able to experiment.

"So she likes change," Nora said. "I can understand that."

"No you can't," Jerry said, "and neither can I. For ten years you've been a teacher. My whole career I've been in advertising."

"I've been a teacher in six different schools," Nora said. "You always seem to forget that."

"Trust me," Jerry said, taking the car about ten miles an hour too fast around a tight curve. "It's different." Then he softened his voice to show Nora he wasn't mad. "Can we talk about something else?"

"Sure," she said, arching her back and gazing through the sunroof at the sky. After awhile she said, "Are you ready for this?"

"Sure," he said, "It'll be fun."

Nora looked at him. "Not the party," she said. "The baby."

"I know," he said. "I meant the baby."

"No you didn't."

Then Nora turned around again to be sure no girls were listening, and she smiled at Jerry. "Liz offered me a free massage."

"Right," Jerry said, playing along. He often couldn't tell when Nora was joking, and he hated to spoil her fun.

"She did," Nora said pulling up her shirt and rubbing her bare belly. "I think I might go tonight at seven."

"That's a really bad idea," Jerry said, gripping the wheel. He realized he was speaking louder than he meant to.

"We thought it was better than me staying there now," she said, "and having her drive me home. Lucy wouldn't want her showing up at the party."

It seemed to Jerry she was serious. "Since when are you two *we*?" he said, forcing himself to watch the road. He figured if they talked about what Lucy wanted, then they might also talk about him.

Nora patted his shoulder. "Honey," she said, "I'm kidding."

As Jerry drove, he wondered what was more terrifying: Lucy becoming a hormonal replica of her mother—or Nora, half-naked, alone in a room with Liz.

"Owwh." Nora flinched and then froze. She put her hand on her side, breathed heavily and rolled her seat back.

"What happened?" Jerry said. "Are you okay?"

"I don't know," Nora said. "I guess that was a contraction."

"No way," Jerry said. "How could that be?"

Nora breathed deeply, in and out through her mouth the way she'd learned in Lamaze.

"That's it. You're definitely not going anywhere. Besides, we said you'd be at the party."

"Those parents just want to know I'll be here overnight," she said. "Like for an emergency."

"What kind of emergency?" he asked. He had never considered the possibility of an emergency.

"Jesus," she said, still accentuating her breathing. "I don't know. Say someone gets her period or something. "Did you look at them. They could *all* get it tonight."

"Now you're talking crazy," Jerry said. He rolled up his window and flipped on the air. "I'll get you a massage next week. I'll get you two massages."

"Jerry, Jesus," Nora said. "I told you I was kidding."

"Kidding about going, or kidding that she offered?"

"Who cares?" Nora said. "I'm not going."

Right then, Jerry saw that his whole life had changed in one summer.

When they pulled into the driveway, Lucy and her friends piled out of the car and dragged their gear onto the front porch. Nora went inside to take a bath while Jerry prepared the food. He figured he'd let the girls get settled before introducing any of his games.

When Nora came back downstairs, it was six o'clock. She poured herself a half a glass of white wine, her weekly ration, then splashed a bit more into the glass.

"When do they leave?" Nora asked.

"Oh, come on," he said. "This will be fun." He kissed Nora on the back of her neck and led her outside.

"One I can handle," she said. "There are six of them." They were running around the yard, flirting with one another and ducking behind the trees.

"Think of this as field research."

"For what?"

"Thirteen years from now."

"But we're having a boy," Nora said. "One boy."

"Just wait," Jerry said. He held a lit match to coals soaked in lighter fluid until fire ripped upward. "One boy can feel like six girls."

Nora put salad and ketchup and mustard on the table on the porch. Jerry grilled veggie burgers and corn, which the girls said they preferred to hot dogs, but they ignored him when he called. After he and Nora ate and went into the house, the girls wandered up, two at a time, and picked at the cold food. Jerry watched from inside, while the orange sun tucked itself behind the faraway trees.

After dinner, the girls settled into their tents and Lucy

came inside to negotiate on their behalf. "You and Nora are staying inside, right?" she said.

"What about ghost stories?" Jerry said, already knowing he was one birthday too late.

"Nora," Lucy said. "Help me."

Nora went over to Jerry and tapped his knees so he would make room for her on the couch. "You're very sweet, Jerry, but she's right. She's too old for games."

"Come here," Jerry said to Lucy. "Give Daddy a hug." He took her hand and pulled her closer. She wore a halter-top and her skin was a milk-chocolaty tan. Jerry rubbed her back. "Remember in the apartment how we used to sit in your teepee in the living room?"

"Sort of," Lucy said, shrugging one shoulder. She looked at Nora.

"You know you're breaking his heart," Nora said to her.

Lucy gave in. "I missed you too, Daddy." She kissed Jerry on the lips, and then went to Nora and kissed her too, on the cheek. "Tomorrow I'll tell you all about camp."

"Okay, okay," Jerry said. "You win. But after your friends go home, I want you all to myself for awhile." Lucy smiled, and Jerry thought maybe she wanted that too. "Tonight, nobody crosses the street. And if it rains, you come inside."

"Thanks Daddy," she said, already halfway to the door.

Nora called to Lucy: "At least get a little sleep."

Jerry leaned back and put his feet on the coffee table. "That was really sweet," he said to Nora. "Thank you."

"She's not going anywhere so fast." Nora kissed Jerry and got up. She took him by the hand, and said: "Now how about the stairs?"

Jerry and Nora lived in an old farmhouse with a big front porch and a two-acre yard, but the hallways were narrow and the ceilings low. When they moved in three years before, they had to cut down the banister to fit their queen-sized bed up the stairs. Since becoming pregnant, Nora had been having premonitions of slipping with the baby and having nothing to grab onto. As her due date got closer, she pestered Jerry to install new balusters and a sturdy oak rail, safety measures she would need before bringing the baby home.

Nora sat cross-legged at the top of the stairs, while Jerry worked at the landing below. He dug the drill bit into the wall and shouted over the grind: "I guess this extra time is good for something."

When the noise stopped, Nora said, "I wouldn't have gone, but I really did want a massage."

From where Jerry was working, Nora's stomach seemed impossibly large.

"A few more minutes," he said, and continued to work.

Nora rubbed her own shoulders, and rocked her head from side to side. Jerry imagined this would be intensely unsatisfying compared to a real massage, in which someone with unlimited patience would rub sweet-smelling lavender oil on her bare body.

"I'm coming up," he said, leaving his tools and the new railing on the floor.

Jerry went into the bathroom and gathered all the folded towels from the wicker stand in the corner. Together with the down comforter and the four pillows on their bed, he made a bundle with a hollow center in which Nora could nestle her belly. She lay face down, and by the time Jerry returned with the oil, she was asleep.

Jerry turned off the bedroom lamp and in the full light of a white summer moon he watched the girls, who now wore just their stretch bras and underwear. As they darted around the yard, he imagined they were long-legged animals, baby deer in a field of clover, but he knew that was not true. They were near-women with flesh they would soon press against young boys, if they hadn't already. No better than a peeping Tom looking out instead of in, he was ashamed. But he didn't look away. He remembered the night Lucy was born, how the crown of her bloody head emerged from between Liz's legs. He had never felt so alone as he had at that moment, and he wondered if he would feel any better during, or after, the birth of a boy.

While Jerry watched the girls, he could see that Nora slept poorly. She moaned every little while, curling and uncurling her knees toward her chest. He wondered how he ever got any sleep, with Nora moving around so much.

At about two-thirty, she opened her eyes.

"Honey?" she said groggily without sitting up. "You're up?"

"Go back to sleep."

"Oh my god," Nora said. "Please tell me you're not spying on them."

"Everything's okay," he said, still facing outside. "Go back to sleep." Jerry noticed his hands and arms looked blue, as though the light from a television shined on them.

Nora moaned. "Jerry," she said. "Tear yourself away. It's time to go." Between contractions, she got up and went to the bathroom.

"Now?" he said. "We can't leave now." When she came back, he still hadn't moved.

Nora pulled down the shade to cover the window. "Jerry," she said. "Look at me. We're having the baby."

"Hang on honey," he said pulling up the shade. "I only count four of them. What if someone ran into the road?"

Nora put on her robe and dialed the phone. "I'm calling Liz."

"Liz?" he said, finally looking at her. "What the hell for?"

"Somebody's going to have to stay with the girls." Then she said into the phone: "Hi, it's me," and she started to cry. "Can you come over? Drive fast, I'm in labor."

Jerry got up and put on his pants. The last person he wanted to see was Liz, but he needed her. Not only was she the mother of one of his children, but like it or not, he and Liz and Lucy and Nora—and now also his unborn son—would be connected for the rest of their lives.

Jerry suddenly needed to shout this out loud. He ran down the stairs and into the yard. The moon, full and high overhead, threw bright light through the trees. His shadow, long and wavy, was distorted on the grass.

"Daddy no," Lucy yelled when she saw him coming. All the girls started screaming and Lucy took off running away.

"Lucy, no," Jerry called. "Come back. It's okay."

As chased her, he wanted to trip and let himself fall. He wanted to feel the wet dew on the front of his t-shirt, and smell damp earth under his face. He wanted Lucy to see him lying there, to come and climb on his back, the way she did when she was small.

He wanted to rear up tall, to roar at the moon, and give her a piggyback ride.

Brent Robison

Family Man

Harold has had it with the squirrels. He's had it with lots of things, but mostly with the squirrels. He tried plywood. They chewed through. He tried wire mesh. They chewed around. He tried mothballs, after Carmine across the street mentioned it over the barbecue. "Like tear gas to the little bastards," Carmine said.

So Harold scattered mothballs all over the attic. They laughed. In Harold's imagination, the squirrels laughed. They pointed their little fingers down through the ceiling at him, clutched their little bellies, and howled.

"I'll kill you," Harold said.

His wife said, "What?" She lay next to him on the bed, not touching. This was the second marriage for both of them. They lay flat on their backs, staring straight up, listening to the scrape and scuffle and scratch of the squirrels in the attic. It was 4:37 a.m.

"Nothing," Harold said.

Harold wears a perpetual suit. On weekends at home he feels oddly naked, as though at a silly costume party. Every Wednesday at noon he gets his shoes shined.

"Whoop-tiddle-ee-dee!" the shoeshine man says. He is a former jazz musician. Harold always gives him a two-dollar tip. Secretly, Harold holds the shoeshine man in high regard, due to his flamboyant way with a rag.

~

It is summer. Harold flips the frisbee to his son with one flick of a stiff wrist. Central Park is in dim twilight. Around them, weeping willows look like the wet walls of a cave.

"I guess opera's not so bad," his son shouts.

The frisbee is an orange neon UFO slicing humid green air. An aria from Turandot booms low thunder from beyond the trees. Over there somewhere in the swarm sit the women: Harold's mother, his sister, his daughter, his second wife.

"Woo, Dad, check it out," his son says, tossing the frisbee under one leg. It's a movement like scissors. The boy looks like his mother, Harold's angry first wife. He's nine and so awkward he can hardly walk.

Harold is not thinking of the frisbee. He's not thinking of the opera. Fireflies wink in spirals.

Harold is thinking of Dolores, the woman he met in the movie line yesterday. Terminator II. Sold out.

Once over dinner, Harold told his first wife, "I had lunch with my new client today. Boy is she gorgeous."

His wife threw the entire pizza at the wall. It was a Domino's medium, delivered hot in under thirty minutes. The door slammed behind her.

"I don't want soup!" his son immediately wailed. The boy was four then and exercised firm control over all meals. He would eat only pizza, plain. Preferably Domino's and never pepperoni, never sausage, only plain. This was a source of great stress in the family, especially at breakfast. Most mornings, Harold felt distinctly relieved as he closed the front door behind him. "Aaah," he would sigh. But at the same time, he felt mysteriously sad. He would murmur, "I am a believer in the principle of ultimate indivisibility. I am a family man."

The boy found a slice with half its cheese and no dust. Harold's daughter, who had been served just before the pie took flight, continued eating. Her eyes blinked once.

His wife spent the night in the bed of the roller-rink boy with the wispy mustache. "We're just friends," she had once told Harold, as she tossed her skates over her shoulder and left for a weekend at the rink.

Harold cleaned up, but a faint brown pattern remained, tomato sauce on green wallpaper. Within a month, his wife had moved into a studio apartment downtown. She said she had to find herself.

For weeks after, Harold could see a picture in the stain. It was a penis with angel wings. This he told no one.

Harold and his second wife wanted a free TV. It was simple—they just had to drive out of their Jersey suburb, head west to the Poconos, listen to a pitch by a perky blonde, tour the Shady Glen condos (offered only to carefully selected married couples with a combined household income over $42,500), and tote their new faux-ebony 13-inch Toshiba home. But they were a mile short of the Delaware when they turned around and went back.

"Bullshit!" Harold said with sincere energy, as loud as he could possibly shout. It was all he could think of to say. It filled the Honda like a light in a closet, on then off. His wife sat. Then she plucked the stylish red glasses off her face, twisted them into a tangle so that one lens popped like a cork into the back seat, and began to cry.

"Oh, good. Another hundred," Harold thought, but he didn't say another word all the way home.

It was because of Harold's kids. It was because Harold's kids were impossible. It was because Harold's kids were so incredibly bad that no second wife could possibly ever have a chance. They were the offspring of Satan and Medusa. They were evil with a capital E. How could a new family ever begin under the weight of such a legacy? All was doom, and messy bedrooms, and backtalk, forever and ever.

When they walked into the house, there was a squirrel in the living room.

M&M's from the bowl on the buffet were scattered all over the floor. Harold's wife's dog, a terrier whose life's purpose should be the murder of rodents, sat looking innocent and bored in the center of the room. The squirrel froze. Then it dashed. It shot like a baseball to the far wall, ricocheted, came back, heading for the stairs, a line drive on a collision course with Harold. It leapt to the couch and into the air, little arms wide, little claws spread, little eyes wild with something so fierce that Harold stopped like he'd been punched. His heart did a flip-flop. His mind heard screams and the crackle of fire. His eyes saw the glare of a beast ready to kill or die in the ancient bloody battle for the cave. This is the way Harold liked to think about it later. But he kept it to himself.

For one second, his mind was blank with terror. Then the squirrel sailed past, scampered up the stairs, and disappeared. "Goddamit!" Harold said. Then he got a poker from the fireplace and stalked up the stairs, walking with very heavy steps.

Standing in the movie line, Harold had noticed right away that the woman in black was alone. He had answered his son's non-stop questions with falsely enthusiastic monosyllables as he watched her, waiting to see if a man would show up at the last minute to dash the hopes that were rising like yeasty dough in his mind. Finally he said, "You an Arnold fan?"

She said, "No; you might say I'm a connoisseur of apocalypse. You know—the end of the world." Her lips were red.

Harold's heart melted. "Aah," he said, nodding with great exaggeration.

"And then the T-1000 morphs right through the bars, it's

so cool!" Harold's son said.

"Morphs?" said Harold.

"Dolores," she said, extending her hand.

In the attic, the squirrels have escalated. They've turned from everyday squirrel routine to orgiastic squirrel celebration. It's a decadent rodent Bacchanalia. They cry out in passion. They scream. They are squirrels with voices! They screech and tumble and gallop up and down in a frenzy of shameless animal abandon. Harold lies in moonlight, mesmerized. He can't be sure if it's joy or pain; if it's love or battle. Or both! It's something altogether alien, surely too exquisite for men. It's sacred squirrel ecstasy.

For a moment, Harold feels guilty for eavesdropping.

"Dad, think fast!" the boy shouts. His face is a round glow in the gray-green twilight of the park, surpassed in luminosity only by the bright cut of the frisbee saucering straight at Harold's head.

"Hey bud, getting a little dark for this, isn't it?" Harold says. Inside, he argues with himself: Aah, Dolores!

Then there's a flash of lightning and a crack of thunder like giant timpani, obliterating the opera beyond the willows. He loosens his tie and makes another awkward toss. He knows that by now the women will have scurried for the car, and his wife will be angry that he hasn't come dashing to save them from the dangerous weather.

"Yowie zowie, Dad!" Rain has begun to fall. The boy does a cartwheel. Little drops, a few, then big drops, a hundred, a thousand. All at once Harold feels himself, unwilled, dribble to a stop. His son stands suddenly still at his side, a skinny shoulder held close by Harold's hand. All they can do is breathe deep together and turn their faces, big and little, to the sky. This feels foolish, but wonderful.

~

Finally, Harold has found the solution. It's simple: rat poison doesn't discriminate among small furry mammals. On a shovel, one by one, Harold carries the stiff little bodies down the stairs to the garbage. His wife won't speak to him. For her, cuteness is a religion. Little animals should frolic on pink wallpaper in the nursery, even an empty nursery.

The squirrels look like the botched homework of a freshman taxidermist: flat hairy things without softness or grace, with sawdust stuffing, and brown teeth too big for their grinning little mouths, and no eyes.

His wife weeps silently. "You'll thank me tonight when you're sleeping like a baby," Harold says.

"No, I won't," she says. "I'll be asleep."

Now, Harold stands stumplike in the drenched clearing, soggy-suited and laughing. His son clings like some twisted miraculous outgrowth of his body, all slimy and whooping in new maleness. The sky has broken! For a moment Harold doesn't care that his wife and mother and sister and daughter are sitting and waiting and growing cruel in a driverless car. For a moment Harold even forgets yesterday. How he had stood there with her too, laughing, entirely mindless of the little boy tugging on his arm. How he had stood there lustful and oblivious in the slanting sun, stood there in his rumpled suit talking to the red lips of a woman dressed in black, just stood there trying desperately to think of all the ways the world can end.

Deborah Artman

BOOK
(a fugue)

1. Now

I work in publishing, we call it a house. We use the word *we*.
We talk about the spine and gutter, widows and signatures. We
say, We'll have to crash the book! We say specs, dummy, proof,
blues, bad break, run in, plates. It has nothing to do with an
accident. I love the smell of a new page, sweet bread. Sometimes
it still feels warm.

~

I sip tea at a coffeeshop counter. A man two seats away is writing
in a book. I pull the book I am reading from my bag, lay the book
on the counter. The man leans over to inspect it.
I've read her! he says. But I couldn't finish—
He smiles.
I read.
I look up when a man sits down next to me and opens a book.
A woman at a table nearby has a book in one hand, her head in the
other. She is enraptured by the baby at the table next to her. She
can't take her eyes off the baby.

~

I meet Oliver, a man I once loved, for a drink. He is tall and
gangly, it's hard for him to fit his knees under the bar table. I'd
met Oliver by the ocean. I was passing through, but he lived there
then. I'd seen his long back tan and slightly stooped. He had a
tendency to hunch. I remember the curve of his back, the spine
like a seam and how desperately I wished to place my palm there.
Now he is wearing a leather jacket, a bit proudly. He looks good,
got that old twinkle, just back from 10 days someplace warm with
his new girlfriend, the 24-year-old. I haven't seen him in months.
I'm running out of money, says Oliver, downing his Absolut and
tonic. I'm in credit-card debt. I've only painted two paintings
since November. I've decided not to do a show this year.
Oliver puts his head in his hands. Ruth, he says, pausing—and in
that pause I am surprised and a bit irritated by the faint flutter of
hope I feel—then he looks up and says, I still haven't figured out
New York.
It takes a while, I say.
What you figure out is that there's nothing to figure out, I didn't
say.
What you figure out is how to *get* out, says my friend Ruben, when
I tell him this story.

Oliver lives in the East Village, talks on the phone, meets people
in bars. He does not work. He tells me it feels strange to be
fucking around.
Why? I say.
I'm 35, says Oliver.
So? I'm 34.
But *you're* not fucking around, he says.
But I *want* to be, I say. I'm just picky.
I tell him about the books I am reading. This story, "Lies," made
me think of you, I say.
Uh-oh, says Oliver.

(It made me think of him because it's about the selectivity of memory. He is one of those people who doesn't remember whole chunks of his past.)
It's about what's left out, I say.

~

Pocket: I have not put my hand here all winter.

~

Ruben and his wife are meeting book deadlines in a house in the country. On weekends, people come to visit them. It helps, says Ruben, to have a third party here. We're under a lot of pressure. His voice on the phone is like honey.
Visitors are nice, I say.
He wants me to visit but I won't go. I tell him about the books I'm reading. I tell him about the young man who interests me.
Poor Ruth, suffering from ageism, says Ruben.
The young man who interests me opens the door for me, I want to tell Ruben. The man who interests me holds open the door.

~

Before I met Oliver for a drink, I waited for him outside my office building. He was late, so I watched the midtown hour of rush. One woman, though, walked slowly. She wore a brown plastic garbage bag. The garbage bag was wrapped around her body: crisscrossed over her breasts, draped over her shoulders, down her back, tied around her waist, like African cloth. She left unwrapped her swollen brown belly: *See my poor and pregnant self.*

~

This book is about a man who has left his wife for a younger
woman. Oliver has left his wife for a younger woman. You will
like this book, I tell him

about the young man who interests me and how I was not able to
seduce him. He wore a baseball hat, I say. He has a deep voice, and
dimples. When he said my name, I wanted
—I couldn't, I say.
See my poor and   self.
Go for it, says Oliver, enthusiastically.
How can you say that? I didn't say.
Before Oliver left his wife for the younger woman, he met me. I
was the bridge, just walk all over

Ruth, have you met anyone? says Ruben. You are in the prime of
your life!

2. Then

There is a game called Book. In this game, each player brings
a book. When it is your turn, hold up the book you've brought
and say the title. Display the cover. If necessary, read out loud a
nugget from the back flap, reveal the publication date. Then every
player except you makes up a first line for the book, writes it on an
index card, which they pass to you. Add to these cards one on
which you have written the true first line. Shuffle the cards. Read
them out loud.

Whoever guesses the correct first line gets a point. If a player's
imagined first line is chosen, he or she gets a point. If no one
chooses the real first line of the book you've brought, you get 5
points. Whoever has the most points after everyone has taken a
turn, wins. Best in groups of 6 to 10.

~

In this painting, a man is skinning an animal, says Oliver.
We are in his studio, by the sea. He is pointing to a picture in a
book.
Oliver explains: This painter is saying that the *painting* is the
skin, and the fact that it is *about* skinning means it is about the
world *below* the skin.

On my walk that day, I see a young girl who is outside in just a
diaper and shirt. She is maybe 2 or 3 years old, standing barefoot
on the front walk to her house. It is October. Why is she outside
dressed like this?
Aren't you cold? I say.
Yeah! she says.
I stop and look up at the house. You should go inside, I say. I
walk away.
Hey! she says. Hey!
The little girl follows me down the street. Hey! she says.
You can't come with me, I say, turning.
Why? says the girl.
Because I'm taking a long walk.
Hey! says the little girl, following me down the street, then
stopping.

~

MY FIRST LINES
1) Spitfires, powerhouses, screen sirens . . . Bette and Joan were
a match made in hell, or Hollywood.
2) I am called Echo of a Laugh, because of my smile, and the Old
Ones will not let me do battle.
3) *Schlep, oy vey, kibbitz*—all Americans speak Yiddish, whether
they know it or not.

4) There is a game called Book.

Who invited Brainy? someone says, as my points add up.
I steal a glance at Oliver.

~

In the wash of fog, when our skins are soft, I lean into Oliver and
taste him, the world below the skin.

~

It is what doesn't happen that fascinates us, the idea of absence,
one night in a bar, absence that coats our tongues like syrup, the
bourbon that loosens the private empty places and the talk of want.
We could make a book! says Oliver, enthusiastically.
We could make a book, I answer. A book of absence. Which, in
my mind, I title: *Makes the Heart Grow Fonder.*
And how to show lack? I say.
The print of lips on the rim of a glass, he says, held up to another's
mouth.
—

A bare foot stepping into someone else's print on the sand, says
Oliver.
Clothes in a heap on the floor, I say. An unmade bed.
—

The blur of a body through a door.

It is our game, defining the space.

~

I read.
I look up.
Hey! says the little girl.

3. Now & Then

Most relationships are like this, says the rabbi at my cousin's wedding in Las Vegas. He takes two books and tilts them so that they lean into each other. The books look like they are kissing. Then one book falls and they both collapse.

Ruben finally pried my secret from me, one night. He made a joke about Oliver and my face opened up, the grief descending, making my cheeks go slack. Ruben took me in his arms: Oh honey, don't you know I love you?

How can you say that? I say to Oliver, when he says Go for it.

I am kneeling on the bathroom floor, elbows on the toilet seat, puking my guts out into the bowl.

In successful relationships, the rabbi continues, the books stand on their own.
He stands the books up, side by side.
I find myself wondering about the space between them. Two inches? One inch? How close is safe?

Ruben curls his body around mine. Everyone needs a mammal, he says, nuzzling my neck.
I drift off to sleep.
Ruben's hand plays at my breast. Ruth's treasures, he says.
Ruth? Are you sleeping?
Almost, I say, listening to Ruben's hand at my breast, what was it saying? What are you doing? I say, my buttocks pressing against

him, answering his hand at my breast. I turn then, to him, blurry, my married friend, a mouth

~

My cousin's wedding is in a hotel. In the middle of the ceremony, as we listen to the words that make a marriage, I suddenly hear music. It sounds like hotel lobby music. *Just slip out the back, Jack.* It *is* hotel lobby music—coming from speakers in the room. The song is "50 Ways to Leave Your Lover." *Make a new plan, Stan.* The tuxedoed best man is doing his best not to laugh. It's too absurd. The rabbi's mouth opens: *Just get yourself free.* Why isn't anyone doing anything about the music? I whisper to the woman sitting next to me, who is my aunt.
I don't know, she says.
I get up, slip out the door, tell every hotel worker I encounter to turn the music off, there's a wedding going

I get up, slip out the door. We won't mention this to anyone, ok? says Ruben, kissing me goodbye

Oliver is holding me on the bathroom floor. I have asked him to come, to help me, to watch. I get up, slip out the door, wiping my mouth

At the reception, people thank me, I am a hero. The Elvis impersonator sings a song to me, kisses me on the neck and tries to pull me on the dance floor.

Ruth, I am worried about you. Why aren't you getting laid? says my friend Danielle.

I dance. I dance with myself. I don't care. I dance with my father. I dance with my brother. You can really dance! says my mother.

Look at Ruth dance! said Ruben at a party. Ruben doesn't dance.

Oliver doesn't dance.

The young man who interests me tells me he only likes to dance slow, but he doesn't

~

My friend Danielle puts her baby down for a nap. She listens to the whimpers, the short cry. Then there is silence. She's down, says Danielle, exhaling. She smiles.

Why is it you put a baby down and you put a book to bed?

~

I read. I look up. There are now three men sitting around me, reading at the counter. At the table, the woman still holds her head in her hand, mesmerized by the baby.

~

In my house today, the book an unmade bed.

Valerie Wacks

)))) ————————————————————————————

Mom's Memoir

"Why don't you write my memoir?" My mother's voice is full
of false cheer, hard as peanut brittle.

It's our first morning together in her Boca Raton condo,
our first visit together since my father died four months ago.
Dutifully, I flew in from New York, to check on her adjustment to
widowhood. My duty as the eldest and only unmarried offspring.
Friday, Saturday, Sunday; Monday morning I could fly back home.
The weekend ahead is a dark ocean, sharks lurking beneath the
surface. I've never known how to talk to her.

"Memoirs are written by the subject. I could write your
biography, but it wouldn't be the same. It would be my story about
your life."

Mom sniffs and pinches her lips together, runs a
manicured hand through short curly hair, currently dyed a pinkish
coppery color. "What's the difference between autobiography and
memoir?"

"I don't know," I say. She always manages to ask
questions that I can't answer.

"You could write the story of my life—whatever you want
to call it. Maybe you'd make some money."

What could be so interesting about her life? Married to a
dentist at an early age, three children raised in a middle class
suburb of Philadelphia, children all go to college, parents retire to
Florida, father dies at age 80, mother is left a financially
independent widow.

We face one another over coffee in the "flamingo room." Sunlight filters through turquoise vertical blinds, creating stripes on the pink walls and the effect is clownish; we could be in a circus tent. The windows are all closed tightly because it's time for the twice-weekly lawn sprinkling. At thirty second intervals, water splatters the side of the house, brown water taken from the murky canal behind us. Earlier, we raced around shutting all the windows so this dirty water couldn't infiltrate onto the rattan furniture upholstered in tropical prints of palm trees and flamingos, or the glass-topped table where we currently sit. I stare at the pink lip of a conch shell centerpiece. I want a cigarette, but I'm sealed in the house. Overhead, a ceiling fan whirs and riffles the pages of the *Boca Gazette*.

I get up to replenish my cooling coffee, walking five feet into the adjoining galley kitchen.

"Why do you always leave the room when I'm talking to you?" my mother says. "And you made too much coffee, enough to last for a week. Such a waste."

"I'll use it later for iced coffee," I say mildly. My stomach clenches and my shoulders ache. Water splatters the kitchen window.

Mom puts on the Weather Channel and crows, "It's 25 degrees and sleeting in New York."

We sit and watch the Weather Channel.

An hour later, we go to the clubhouse and pool, walking past identical little houses of pink stucco with white shutters, single-car garages. Everyone has a garage-door opener here. Identical little lawns, the blades of thick stubbly grass glistening with the recent obligatory sprinkling, puddles dot the row of macadam driveways. A white ibis stands on one leg by a fuchsia jacaranda, its neck long and graceful, its beak long and orange.

"I love it here. It's so peaceful, so orderly, everything taken care of," Mom says.

The sky is now mostly grey, big soft clouds scud against one another in a humid breeze. There's a small lake in the center of the condo complex, more houses and a sidewalk ringing the lake where elderly people in athletic togs walk or slowly bicycle. Mom waves, or pauses to introduce me. I smile at the wrinkled faces and feel exhausted. Could I be jet-lagged from a New York to Florida flight?

I walk down the concrete steps into the low end of the swimming pool. The water is unrefreshingly warm. Mom is already immersed to her thighs, chatting with a lavender-haired friend.

"Her hair!" The woman points at me. "She needs a cap."

"Pool regulations say you need a bathing cap if your hair is shoulder-length or longer. People will complain," Mom says.

My hair barely brushes my shoulders. "I won't dive under," I say, and breast-stroke off into the tepid chlorinated water. It stings my eyes.

An intermittent sun appears. Dripping, I heave myself onto a lounge chair and stretch out to savor the rays. I close my eyes and try not to listen to the 1940's pop music blaring from the clubhouse speakers.

"What are you doing?" Mom barks by my ear. "The sun is very strong here, you'll burn, you'll get skin cancer, you'll wrinkle like a toad."

"Which is worse?" I don't open my eyes. Is she trying to hex me?

"Very funny. Put this on, it's sunblock #75, total block. I always use it when I'm exposed. Oh, Miriam—this is my oldest child, Francine."

I lever up on one elbow, squint at a short portly woman with very white, very even teeth—must be new dentures, and a skirted leopard print bathing suit over marbled thighs. No doubt, my future.

"Pleased to meet you," I say.

"You'll get a sunburn," Miriam replies.

"What did I tell you?" My mother says.

I smile and close my eyes.

We spend the next two mornings at the pool. I attend an exercise class with Mom in the clubhouse, meet more of her friends, and feel both guilty and triumphant at how easily I can bend my head to my knees. Afternoons are spent shopping, running errands, seeing bargain matinee movies. Mom complains about my refusal to drive and how I let her chauffer me around. The highways here are clogged with elderkochers crawling in Lincoln Continentals and impatient youths tail-gating and lane-cutting in hip-hop throbbing convertibles. You've got to be on drugs, prescription or otherwise, to drive around here.

"I live in the city, Mom. I take taxis," I say.

"You're so dependent, still a child. You want everyone to do for you."

I grit my teeth. "Your turn signal is still on."

"Maybe I want to make another turn," she says. But she turns off the signal.

On our last evening together, we sit out on Mom's back deck overlooking the canal. We sit on white plastic chairs, our glasses of white wine sweating onto a white plastic table. Tiny geckos dart up and down a nearby lime tree. The air is soft and has an acrid scent from the pesticide spraying done that morning. Not surprisingly, there are no mosquitoes. An insect is a rare wildlife sighting, probably a mutant. Huge lavender and peach clouds collide in the sky. A mottled black and white duck with scabrous red wattles glides down the canal. The ceaseless whoosh of traffic provides our auditory backdrop.

I light a cigarette and wait for the inevitable lecture and silently count the hours until I can excuse myself for bed, then board a plane the next morning.

Mom just sighs and fans the smoke away. Then she replenishes her glass of wine.

"It's hard to be alone after 48 years of marriage. I get lonely, frightened even. I have trouble sleeping."

I nod, although I'd only been married once for less than three years. Mom isn't looking at me for a change, anyway. I draw deeply on my cigarette. She sips her wine.

"You know, our marriage was not entirely happy. Your father and I often did not get along."

I nod again. I knew. I'd heard plenty of late night quarrels when I was young. Afterwards, Dad would come into my room, sit on the edge of my bed and tell me about his problems with Mom. It made me uneasy, but also, I was proud to be his confidante, to be Daddy's favorite.

Mom gazes at the canal where now, three ugly ducks bob serenely. "Don't feed them. They're beggars, they'll come right up to the house."

"I won't."

"After the children were born, our sex life was never the same. Oh, he'd go through the motions, but it was just a performance. I thought it must be my fault, I'd become unattractive."

"You were beautiful, Mom. I've seen the pictures." Oops—too much past tense. "You're still very attractive," I add.

She still isn't looking at me.

"I'll never let another man into my life, never let myself be dominated and criticized that way." She glares into her glass of wine.

This is embarrassing; being Mom's confidante was never my family role. "Sure, you don't need to. You're well off, you can relax and enjoy your new life, learn about yourself as an independent person." My attempt to be supportive sounds pretty lame. Luckily, Mom's not paying attention.

"I'll never be with a man again," she says slowly. "But I was with a man once. I mean a man other than your father."

I sit up straighter in my chair, the plastic slats gripping my bare thighs.

"It was when we were doing 'Fiddler on the Roof', just an amateur production. You remember, your father was the butcher, but I had a bigger role. I was Tzeitel, Tevye's oldest daughter." Mom pauses to sing, "Matchmaker, matchmaker, make me a match. Find me a find, catch me a catch." Her voice is raspy, but strong and in tune.

"I remember. I was sixteen, just got my license and I drove to the show in your Chevy Impala, what a gas guzzler. Who was your—who was he?"

"He played the poor tailor, I forget his name, my love interest." Mom smirks, or maybe not. The sky has deepened, a couple of stars twinkle and a plane roars overhead. I pour both of us more wine.

"But I remember his real name. It was Ben." Mom savors the name in her mouth like a chunk of Belgian chocolate. "Ben. He was married, too."

"Did you meet in motels?" I light another cigarette and picture Mom some 35 years ago, her hair dark then and shellacked into a Jackie Kennedy do. A cinderblock roadside motel with flashing neon lights, checking in under an assumed name, a diaphragm stowed in her patent leather handbag. This is harder to imagine.

"Yes. And one time, I had him over for dinner when his wife was away. You were all there. Do you remember?"

I try, but nothing comes. My parents had many friends and gave frequent dinner parties. The guests were all noisy, boring grown-ups to me. "No, I can't picture him. How long did it last?"

"Almost a year, and it was wonderful. But I didn't like the sneaking around, didn't like to think of myself as that kind of woman, so I broke it off. Even the ending was my choice. Your father never knew. Do you think it was terrible?"

I look at her lined face, her thinning hair, everything grey in the waning dusk. "No. I think it was fine and nobody was hurt." And I can picture that younger woman, clad in a peasant skirt, a bright shawl around her shoulders, dark eyes glowing as she sings, "Matchmaker, matchmaker."

"Yes. I think it was fine." I lean forward and briefly touch Mom's gnarled, soft hand.

The next morning, I pack my bags and make coffee in the electric drip. Mom comes out in a bright pink terrycloth robe and matching slippers.

"It's too much, enough to last for weeks, such a waste." She pauses. "But actually, it's nice to wake up to the smell of fresh coffee."

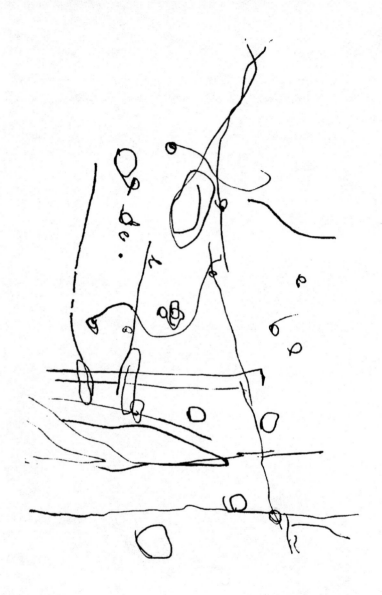

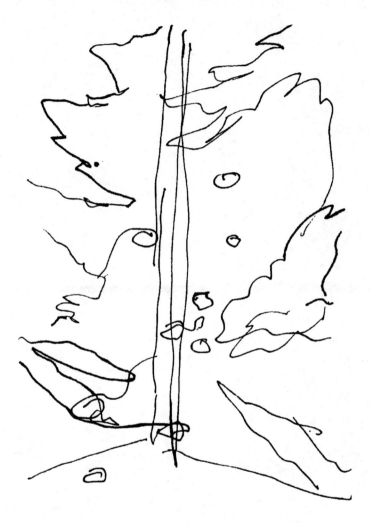

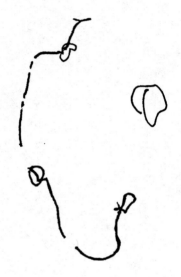

Fireflies
Carol Field

Thomas H. Brennan

》》────────────────────────────

The Crying Buddha

On March 2, 2001, when the Taliban destroyed the two Buddhas, Shamama and Salsal, in the Bamiyan Valley in central Afghanistan, the largest Buddha in the western hemisphere cried. Carol E. Baxter, a recent widow, witnessed it alone on that sunny Friday afternoon just before three. If it weren't for the physical destruction, her story would have been quite unbelievable.

It all started the previous rainy Sunday when, on a whim, she attended a vegetarian luncheon open to the public at the Chuang Yen Monastery in the town of Kent, New York. At the end of the meal, one of the monks, a small, wiry man with a close shaved head, garbed in a simple steel-gray tunic, approached the lectern at the front of the refectory, tapped on the microphone and informed the diners that there was still room for anyone wishing to attend the week-long retreat—The Quest for Enlightenment.

On another whim, she signed up. After lunch she returned to her home in Cold Spring, several miles away to the west, gathered some clothes for the week, asked her neighbor to feed her two cats, and returned to the monastery. She parked outside Yin-Kuang Hall where her Spartan room contained only a bed, a chair, a small table with a lamp and a sitting Buddha in the corner of the room.

The retreat started at five o'clock in the Pu-Tuo-Shan memorial room in the library. There were seven other retreatants, four of whom were Japanese Buddhist monks. Dr. Ming R. Shen, a

93

renowned scholar in Zen Buddhism who had studied under D.T. Suzuki, read several passages from the writings of Prince Siddhartha Gautama—the Buddha before his own awakening. He recited the writings in a slight accent but slowly enough, with crisp enunciation, so that she identified immediately with the travails of the prince; he sought meaning in his own life and in his unavoidable death.

Siddhartha said, "Before my awakening I was overwhelmed with my own sorrow, with my own aging, with my own weakness, with my own inevitable death. Is there a reason I should live and not die? I will seek the unsorrow, the unaging, the unweakness, the undying that is within me. I will awaken to the sacred I; I will awaken to mine own true self." It reminded her of Shakespeare.

Her husband's death in a tragic accident only a month ago left Carol confused; on one hand she felt relief from his abuse but, on the other hand, guilt at her rejoicing in his death. On the evening of the last day of January, on his trip home from skiing in the Adirondacks, he exited from the Taconic Parkway onto Route 301 West toward Cold Spring. The road had turned slightly slick at dusk. The police reconstructed the accident and determined he made the turn too sharply; it was just like him to do this, she remembered. How many times had she asked him to slow down on that hairpin ramp? One time he said to her, "Pull your seat belt tighter," and laughed.

"Put yours on," she replied.

He laughed again—at her weakness; quickly, he abandoned his morbid joviality: "Look bitch, don't ever tell *me* what to do."

He had lost control of the car, sending it into a tree, which severed it neatly in half. The two disjointed parts bounced through the brush like children skipping in a meadow. The driver's side door and Mr. Baxter remained plastered to the tree, the steering wheel spinning on his out-stretched arm. Her two children, Arthur who lived in San Diego and Emily who lived in

Seattle, refused to attend the funeral. Each, however, extended invitations to their mother to come and stay as long as she liked. She had declined and neither had called in the month following their father's death. They both told her it was she who now had to make decisions; they had already made theirs.

At the gravesite her pastor, Monsignor Scalon, aware of her trials, whispered to her, "Perhaps it is God's will."

She stared back at him and replied, "He's a bit slow in deciding, isn't he? Now that the damage has been done."

Dr. Shen led the retreatants each morning in a slow, high pitched chant of mantras with many "o" sounds, and lectured to them before lunch about the levels of awakening. The daily lunch was similar to the Sunday lunch; brown rice sprinkled with bits of spinach and arugula, tofu, chopped zucchini, eggplant and kale. The prayer before lunch warned the diners neither to like the food nor dislike it; food existed for the sustenance of the body only. It would be difficult for Carol to do the former but easy to do the latter, yet by Wednesday her cleansed taste buds adjusted to the bitterness of the kale and the smoothness of the tofu.

Dr. Shen met with each retreatant briefly in the early afternoon for as long as it took to stroll around Seven Jewels Lake; sometimes he extended the walk, indicating one of the teak benches along the shore where they would sit. Sometimes they paused on the bridge over the neck of the lake, with Dr. Shen dropping small purple petals into the water, and sometimes they sat on The Chair of Two Stones. A pair of mute swans, early arrivals from wintering on the Hudson, patrolled the far edge of the lake searching for suitable nesting grounds. After the midday consultation the remainder of the afternoon was reserved for solitary meditation, and he recommended that some portion of the afternoon be spent in The Hall of the Ten Thousand Buddhas.

By the time Friday afternoon arrived Carol's trust in the wisdom of Dr. Shen grew; through the week he listened carefully to her stories of abuse, holding his hand behind his ear and cupping it so he didn't miss a syllable. Although the details of her rocky marriage resembled many stories he had heard before, his concentration on her words encouraged her to speak with more particulars. He asked a pointed few questions and was most interested in their meals—what foods they chose, what meats, what fish, and how they were prepared; baked, broiled or sautéed. When they were sitting in The Chair of Two Stones she told him about how she and her husband ate dinner; the two of them at a large dining room table, she reserved with eyes down, he overbearing with malevolent stares, and his reaching over to her, pricking her hands and arms with his fork to solidify his power and authority over her. When Dr. Shen heard this he placed his fingers on his lips, indicating she should stop and be silent. He delicately placed one of her hands in his, pushed up the sleeve of her blouse, and stroked her arm up and down in spiral motions. He whispered, "The remnants of pain will leave through the fingertips and when they meet the air they will dissolve. Point your hands upward to the Buddha and he will instruct you on how to wash the pain, how to wash, how to wash the pain from within you." His hands were warm, his impeccably clean fingernails closely clipped, and his touch easy and non-threatening. Afterwards she remembered that he had said the phrase "how to wash" three times.

They rose from The Chair of Two Stones and completed their walk around the lake. "Tomorrow we shall part," he said to her. "We are taught to choose what is certain and avoid what is uncertain, but the Buddha sees differently; choose life even though it is uncertain; do not choose death even though it is certain. We are all punished with the certainty of death—even the Buddha."

They had reached the beginning of the path around Seven Jewels Lake. "You are Christian?" Dr. Shen asked. Carol nodded.

"Even the Christ died," he said.

"But he rose," she replied.

"That is the mystery," he said. "Sadly, the Christ lived after the Buddha, otherwise this would certainly be the first question he would put to Jesus."

So on that Friday afternoon Carol was in the Hall of the Ten Thousand Buddhas when the Taliban ignored international pleas and shelled the ancient Buddhas into desert dust. The architecture of the Hall imitated the style of the Tang Dynasty. The entire structure contained no internal pillars, only seven eighty-foot arches, thus creating a spacious, unobstructed interior. The ceiling was empty, unmarred by distractions; the necessary lights were recessed into the corners of the hall behind sliding teak walls. The axis of the hall was east-west with the eastern wall constructed almost entirely of glass; even the doors were glass with glass handles. The thirty-seven foot white marble Buddha Vairocana dominated the western wall, surrounded by ten thousand Buddhas sitting on a lotus terrace. The white marbled Buddha gazed serenely into the darkening eastern sky with dry eyes.

Carol slipped off her strapless sandals and entered the hall. One monk organized books on a table in a corner of the hall. Another monk replaced the fruit in the Ming bowl at the foot of the Buddha, fresh oranges and tangerines, and lit another stick of incense. Without speaking they came together at the foot of the Buddha, bowed in unison, and left by the door near the altar where the colored porcelain statue of Kuan-Yin Bodhisattva sat. Carol and the Buddha remained alone.

She picked up a saffron-yellow prayer cushion, walked to the center of the hall and bowed to the Buddha. She stepped backwards still facing the Buddha and placed her cushion behind the abbot's cushion and slightly to its left. She sat down in the lotus position, closed her eyes and began her prayer for the second pattern of enlightenment, the *yoniso manasikara*, the wise reflection on the issues of one's own life that are worth paying attention to, but more importantly, the ones to be ignored. In her hand she held a small book, *The Songs of Milarepa*. She opened the book randomly and read, "Evil karma is like a waterfall, which I have never seen flow upward."

Dr. Shen had repeatedly advised Carol not only to prioritize, but to banish those issues of the soul that are entirely capable of inner destruction merely by being present in the mind. It was hard at first for her to banish her husband's memory; she discovered it difficult to let go of her hatred but gradually during the week she had come to the realization that her future would be with her children and she decided to go to them. The fruition of this new reality allowed Carol to breathe more slowly, and her fingers tingled as the evil issues evaporated from her skin. Her mind cleared and the image of her husband became harder to visualize; he was dying now in her eye's mind. Her lips moved slightly as if beginning a smile but stopped as if they had forgotten how to form one. She closed the book, looked up into the Buddha's face and saw the first tear forming in the Buddha's right eye.

At first she thought the Buddha's tear was a reflection of a happy tear in her own eye and she wiped her eyes with a tissue, but the tear did not vanish. She then thought the tear was a reflection from the glass wall into the Buddha's eye, but it grew. She thought finally it was her imagination, but the tear was real. It expanded from the Buddha's cornea near the bridge of his nose toward his iris. As the tear developed, the heaviness of the water formed an arc at the bottom of the tear. When its radius reached a foot, a second tear appeared in the Buddha's left eye and expanded in the same manner. The first tear soon covered the entire Buddha's eye and emanated from the eye, forming a gargantuan bubble. It shook and wobbled then separated from the eye, and rolled down the Buddha's cheek. Inside the tear Carol saw the image of another Buddha, tall and tan; then the tear dropped off and the Buddha in the tear exploded. The tear struck the Buddha's knee and spattered into ten thousand droplets, but knocking to the floor only one of the small Buddhas sitting on the lotus terrace. It also broke into ten thousand pieces. The water flowed off the lotus terrace like a waterfall, cascading onto the floor, soaking the rugs and Carol's prayer cushion, leaking through the pine floor boards into the gift shop below. She stood and the water covered her feet up to her ankles. Her socks were soaked. The water was cold and sent ice pangs up her shins.

Carol looked up into the second tear. It too contained a tan Buddha but taller than the first. It too exploded and the second tear dropped directly onto the ceremonial table holding the incense and the Ming bowl with the fresh fruit. It split the table in half and then burst upward like a geyser spraying the entire hall with a fine mist. Water dripped from the mural of "The Pure Land of the Amitabha Buddha" hanging on the north wall and ran the paint in the mural of "The Eastern Paradise" on the south wall. No more tears appeared, but where the Buddha's skin under the eyes had been smooth there were now sag lines in the white marble.

The two monks who had left Carol alone rushed back into the hall, lifted their robes, and waded through the water toward her. In their confusion they spoke to her rapidly in Chinese. She was dripping wet. She turned upward once again to the Buddha and wondered if, like the Christ, he also baptized.

Jasmine Tsang

The Cockfight

~ Shanghai, 1937 ~

When Glorious Peace did not show up for his visit from their ancestral home in Hangzhou, his brother, Glorious Dragon, knew exactly where to find him. Dragon charged up the stairs of a tenement house and barged into his brother's favorite opium den. He pushed aside the proprietor and screamed obscenities against the nauseating, sweet smell of opium smoke. No one dared to stop him.

He yanked up some gaunt torsos hunched over the miniature hurricane lamps, cursing each one before throwing them back to their lolling positions. The wasted figures groaned and stared up at him with vacant eyes, too debilitated to protest. He kicked aside a lacquered screen, and found Peace in the private alcove. His brother protested in unintelligible moans, while saliva dribbled from his gaping mouth, full of yellow, smoke stained teeth. Shouting profanities, Dragon dragged his brother like a damp rag into a waiting car and brought him directly to a clinic.

The treatment began. Dragon called his brother almost every day. He asked the same questions in the respectful tone that was expected from a younger brother.

"Brother Peace, how are you?"

"I'm fine." The answer was usually curt and surly.

"Brother Peace, is the clinic treating you well?"

"The food is inedible."

"I'll talk to the nurses and have some restaurant food sent in to you. You just tell them what you want."

"I have no appetite, so don't bother!"

"Brother Peace, please try to concentrate on getting better. You'll need strength to fight your addiction."

A long silence. "My hands still shake. I want to go home."

Dragon coughed to mask his discomfort. "When you're better, I'll come to take you to the train. I promise you."

The conversation seldom varied. Sometimes Dragon volunteered information about their family in Hangzhou, but Peace never asked. When prodded, he would respond that he had received letters from their sister, Purple Jade, but his attitude was always hostile and his voice gruff, as if none of that should be his brother's concern.

Weeks passed. Dragon went to fetch his brother when it was time for his discharge. Since the train to Hangzhou did not leave until the afternoon, they needed to while away a few hours. Dragon could not think of any common interest. He loved American movies, but his brother did not understand English. He could take Peace for a drink, but it was still morning and he did not want to send his brother home inebriated. Going to the race course might have killed some time, but there was no racing that morning. Dragon finally settled on going to a cockfight in the old Chinese section of town where it was featured as lunch time entertainment.

The cockfight was held in the courtyard of an ancient Chinese mansion, lately turned into a restaurant. A sand area had been set up in the center of the tiled courtyard, with a rope defining its boundaries. Rickshaw-pullers and peddlers in their rough cotton Chinese suits squatted behind the rope. The office workers in their shirts and ties, and shop keepers in their fine Chinese jackets and baggy pants sat or leaned from the banisters of the covered walkway surrounding the courtyard. Dragon looked like an Oxford student in a three-piece gray wool suit. Peace was dressed in a blue silk gown, lined with white silk collar and cuffs. People made way for the distinguished looking pair and they edged into two spaces, leaning on the banister.

The restaurant was similar in architecture to the family mansion in Hangzhou, and the casual, raucous atmosphere was certainly not intimidating. Dragon congratulated himself on the choice.

The two roosters and their handlers were already in their opposing places. One handler was busy preparing his bird. He slurped mouthfuls of water from a porcelain bowl beside him. Holding up the rooster to face away from him, he squirted the water on the rooster's back and wings. He groomed the brown feathers and dark green iridescent tail until luminous, then cradled the bird like a baby, all the while stroking its neck. The other handler looked fierce and alert, standing with his unusual black rooster with distinctive white shiny accents tucked under his right armpit. His left hand stroked the black plumage. The combatants swiveled their heads, flashing their fiery red combs, and jerked their necks up and down, scanning the battlefield.

As if on cue, both handlers took out glistening blades and capped them onto the spurs of their fighters. People stirred. They argued whether one bird's eyes were spitting fire more fiercely than the other and compared the spirit of the upright tails. They clucked and shouted out the odds.

Dragon bet a few yuan on the one with brown feathers and green tail, but his brother smiled and bet heavily on the black one.

"Have you gone to any cockfights in Hangzhou?"

"No," Peace scowled. "These people are all so rough and uncouth!"

Yes, Dragon thought, his brother had been thoroughly trained in the Confucian classics, and the snobbery of gentility. No doubt their father would share the same opinion. "It's exciting to scream and shout sometimes," said Dragon. "I forget my frustrations."

Soon the roosters were thrust toward each other, and the

handlers clucked and called to provoke them. People all around flapped their arms, shouted, and made strange croaking sounds to inflame the fighting cocks. Dragon turned to the brown cock, "Oh, you coward, jump on him! Jump on him!" Both contestants drew blood. Peace turned away and tugged on his brother. "I can't stand all this savagery and noise!"

Dragon lingered. He was deep into the game, cursing and cheering. "We'll forfeit our entrance fee!"

"I'll wait for you in the restaurant." Peace left, sweeping the long loose sleeves of his Chinese robe over his brother's Western suit. Dragon followed immediately; he did not want to lose his brother again. "Let's have lunch. I'll ask the waiter to collect our winnings. One of us will win for sure, but your black one holds the better odds!"

"Brother Dragon, you are too Westernized! A young man from our book-fragrant family should never shout and curse the way you did!"

Dragon was still wiping sweat from his brow. "Cockfighting is a Chinese game. What does being Westernized have to do with it?"

"Cockfighting is entertainment for the rickshaw-pullers and common peddlers! You are not supposed to join them."

"You're lecturing me about proper manners after I fished you out of an opium den?" Dragon spoke heatedly. "So now you're ashamed of me for enjoying a cockfight?"

"I am still your older brother!" Peace sat down in the restaurant, thumping on the table, demanding service. "You better not let our father know how you're comfortable with such brutality!"

"Plenty of people here look respectable enough to me! Oh gentility and harmony," he jeered. "I suppose it is all right to have any family disgrace so long as outsiders don't know anything about it!"

Peace ignored the sarcasm, and calmly ordered his favorite dishes. He lectured his brother as if he were a child.

"You have swallowed your Western learning whole! Everyone is equal to you. There is no clear definition of what is refined and what is coarse behavior. If more people enjoy killing and carousing, then that is popular and fine too! You should follow the example of our ancient sages and behave like a Confucian gentleman!"

"I don't enjoy killing anything! What's wrong with my Western education? The missionaries taught us peace and charity."

"Yes, they seduce you with good words, but they'll do anything to gain the advantage in trade. Look at me! I can't live without the pipe." His eyes moistened. "They pushed opium into our country!"

Dragon was surprised to hear his brother acknowledge the evil possessing him. "I'm sorry if I haven't behaved like a younger brother with due respect toward you, but you are supposed to be cured now, and you mustn't go back to the poison!"

Tears came streaming down his cheeks, Peace wiped his face with the hot towel the waiter brought. "I'm a weakling!" He cried into the towel. "How can you be strong when everything has been turned upside down?"

"What do you mean?" Dragon was frightened to see his usually stoic brother lose control.

"I was taught to be humble, never to prate about our connections, our abilities. The Western traders stick out their chests, strut their pride, brag and promise heaven and earth. How can I believe them? How can I do business with them? I was taught grace in bending low, showing respect and obedience to our traditions. The Westerners swagger with the wealth they won from us, and glory in their firearms and power!" His red face emerged from the towel with all the fury of a helpless man.

"You are certainly correct." Dragon was eager to calm him. "However, don't you think our old culture has been too successful in repressing you and our sister? They forced you to memorize the classics, bound her feet, and denied you the freedom to explore and learn from the new order . . ."

"Yes, perhaps," Peace hid his face behind the towel again. "I'm weak. I'm a weakling. What can I do? The pipe helped me shut out the noise, the confusion."

The waiter came to inform them that the black rooster had won and handed them the money. He was quickly dismissed to bring them their food.

The waiter's presence calmed the brothers. Both gazed steadily into each other's eyes and nodded. The winnings were large enough to pay for the meal plus a handsome tip. Even Peace managed a smile.

At the train station, Dragon offered his hand, but his brother refused to shake it. Instead, he bowed in the traditional way. "No, no, no, younger brother Dragon, you have saved my life again. Allow me to show my respect."

Glorious Dragon was moved, but inside, he seethed and cursed the tyranny of their old traditions that still held his brother as a humble, obedient weakling. Still, he was surprised by the expression of gratitude. Would he know where to find his brother the next time? He returned the bow.

Maia Rossini

Tuck's House

It wasn't too far to walk, but my husband and I decided to drive to Tuck's. It was barely spring and the winter had been long and hard, blowing itself out in one last April blizzard. The snow had taken a long time to melt. The earth was still soggy with ice water and the green patches were few and bright against the dull muddy color of the rest of the ground. I wore a short skirt that exposed my newly pinked legs. In spite of winter hanging on for so long, the day had been warm and I'd spent most of it naked on our back porch, feeding my skin's craving for sun. I stayed stretched out until the trees started casting shadows on my bare ass, then I went inside, brushed my hair, polished my nails and dug out my spring skirt. It was pink, just a shade lighter than my legs turned out to be.

My husband turned up into the driveway of Tuck's new house. The driveway was narrow and steep and unpaved. The wheels of the car spun a little in the mud and gravel, but my husband was a good driver and we made it up to the top of the hill without getting stuck.

Tuck had struck a bargain with this new house. He didn't own an inch of it, but in Tuck's mind it was already his. He had been given the job as caretaker for an indefinite amount of time. The original owners had died and the heirs wanted to sell, but with times being what they were, there weren't many people who were interested in buying something this big. Tuck figured he had at least a few years before the economy would pick up again. Until then, he called the place Manor de Tuckman.

We parked at the edge of a meadow and got out of the car. There were stone steps cutting through the grass, leading even further up the hill to the house itself. Apparently the rich even get to enjoy the thaw first, because the meadow was already bright green and spotted with purple and yellow flowers. If you looked over to the west you could see the Hudson River and the sunset. The house was insanely beautiful in the sunset light. It was stone and brick and it spiraled four stories into the sky. There were two towers with pointed green copper roofs, and at least twenty huge windows, the glass so old that you could see bubbles and ripples, some stained glass, too, and crawling vines of leafless ivy zig-zagging up and down the walls. It looked like every light in the house was on. I could see a huge chandelier burning through the bottom floor windows.

Looking at that house made me want to cry. Up until last week Tuck had been freeloading off of us, sleeping on our living room floor. We had a one-bedroom cabin with nothing going for it but a back porch and a view of the highway. Tuck had simply answered an ad in the local paper. He hadn't even known the folks who owned this place. It had been that easy.

This party was Tuck's housewarming. He had invited all his old janitor friends from the Culinary Institute. That was where he worked until they fired him for making a pass at one of the student chefs. Of course, Tuck's wife Joey found out why he got fired and threw him out on the street. My husband, who knew Tuck from before Tuck dropped out of school, felt sorry for him and I always liked Tuck okay, so I said he could stay with us for a while.

It had been fine at first. Tuck had been real polite, always doing the dishes and sweeping the floors and stuff, but that didn't last long. He got lazy and little things started to get to me. He had to have a new towel every time he bathed, which was about twenty times a day; he couldn't bother to lift the lid on the kitchen trash can, so garbage just piled up on top of it. Pretty soon, he stopped offering to help clean anything. He picked up his bedding every day and that was it. I was relieved when he finally told us he was leaving. I thought we were going have to kick him out. But now that I saw the house I wished him back on our living room floor again.

The front door was thick and dark and had cherubs carved into the corners. There was a huge brass knocker shaped like a bird sitting on top of a rose. I lifted it and let it fall against the door. We could hear the steady thump of a bass guitar pounding through the door. We waited and knocked again, louder this time. After another minute, a skinny girl with blond, shaggy hair answered. She was wearing a shrunken black tee shirt that showed her navel and had a red satin heart stitched on the front. She bent and straightened her knees in time with the music.

"Oh, hi," she yelled, "you guys here for the party, right?" She turned around. "Hey! Hey, Tuck! Tucker! Tuckman! Some folks are here!"

Tuck rounded the corner into the entryway. "Oh hey! Yeah, it's my old roomies!" He stepped between us and put his arms around us, pulling us close. "Yeah, well, whaddya think, huh? No offense or anything but sure as hell beats sleeping on your floor, huh?"

I looked at the ornately carved hat rack in front of me. It was cherry wood. I bit the inside of my cheek. Tuck took his arms off our shoulders and grabbed the blonde. "This is Teresa, guys," he said.

"Hey," she said. I noticed she was wearing yellow plastic barrettes shaped like ducks.

We followed them into a room with parquet floors and a huge iron chandelier lit with about a hundred candles. The ceilings must have been twenty feet high. I hit my husband on the arm. "Look at this place," I muttered. He whacked me back and nodded.

I couldn't stand it. I said, "Tuck, where's the bathroom?"

Tuck laughed. "Which one? There's a dozen or so."

"I hate you," I said under my breath.

The bathroom had two sinks, a clawfoot tub that could fit three people, and a separate room for the toilet, which had one of those pull chains that hang from the ceiling. The whole room smelled like expensive perfume. I sat on the toilet for a long time just thinking about how great it would be to live in this house and how much Tuck didn't deserve his good luck. I also thought that Teresa the barrette girl would undoubtedly be getting to move in and live with Tuck and that I hated her too. I flushed the toilet about a million times just so I could yank that chain.

Everyone was in the kitchen when I came back out. There were two kegs of beer. "German!" yelled Tuck proudly. Tuck was passing out hollowed out cigars filled with bud. My husband nudged me and handed me a cigar when I walked in. "You should hear how much they're paying him to stay here," he said. I put the cigar in my purse and accepted another from Tuck a few minutes later.

"Hawaiian!" said Tuck.

"Great," I said. I grabbed a handful of tortilla chips. "So, Tuck," I said with my mouth full, "what are you going to do with all this time on your hands?"

Tuck inhaled and smiled. "I don't know," he said still holding the smoke in. "Kick back, relax, play a little croquet on the back lawn, maybe swim in my spring-fed swimming pool." He exhaled. "Whatever it is the leisure class does."

"Right," I said. I walked back over to my husband. He was talking to a short, fat guy with a handlebar mustache. I held the stogie to my lips. "Light me up, honey," I said.

I was walking barefoot down a hall. I was on the third floor. Most everyone in the party was still down in the kitchen, just a few scattered people drifting into the dining room and back porch. The third floor was where the smaller bedrooms were. I had looked at four so far. Two had adjoining bathrooms, three had walk-in closets. They were all at least the size of my living room, dining room, and kitchen put together. The carpet felt like velvet under my feet. It had roses and birds and trees on it. I cupped my hand under my joint so I wouldn't ash on the rug. Not that Tuck would care. This was not something Tuck would even think about. At the end of the hall was a sitting room, a solarium, I guess you would call it. It had leaded glass windows from floor to ceiling. It was filled with plants. It had French doors that led out onto a balcony.

I looked at the plants. There were flowers I had never seen, and some sort of white and pink ivy twining around the edges of the windows and cascading down practically to the floor. Some of the plants were already drooping, turning brown at the edges of their leaves. I swore when I touched a fat white flower and it fell off into my hand. Tuck probably hadn't even been in this room since he moved in. All of these plants would be dead in a month.

I went back out to the hall and got a big vase that was on a side table. It was white with tiny painted violets and so delicate that I could see the shadow of my hand through it. I took it into one of the bathrooms and filled it with water, then I went back into the solarium and started watering all the plants. It took me a long time, at least three trips back into the bathroom, to finish. I had to stand on a chair to reach some of the plants, but I dusted off my feet before I climbed up. I kept smoking the whole time. I put the ash into one of my shoes that I was carrying with me.

When I was done I stood back and looked at all the plants. They already looked better to me. "You're welcome," I said out loud. Then I felt stupid talking to plants so I went outside onto the balcony.

The balcony was fixed up so you could be out there in any type of weather. The roof hung over really far. It looked out onto the swimming pool and onto a bunch of huge lilac bushes. They were just tipping green. I imagined that the people who used to live in this place sat on the balcony a lot. It was a lover's balcony. It was a goddamned Romeo and Juliet balcony. I knew that people had played music under this balcony. That men had made declarations. That girls had accepted them. I loved this balcony.

I thought that after Tuck killed the plants he'd be sure to ruin this balcony some way, too. He'd probably set up a hibachi on it. He'd lay his wet underwear over the railings to dry.

Past the swimming pool were rolling hills of perfectly cut grass that reached all the way down to the river. I could see the silhouettes of deer grazing. I tried to imagine the kind of people who must have lived here. What it would have felt like to have this kind of money, to own this kind of house. Looking down I felt a little dizzy so I took one last drag on my joint and carefully stubbed it out on the bottom of my shoe. I deposited the remains in my purse. I went back downstairs.

Everyone was dancing in the dining room. They had pushed back this massive carved wood table and rolled back the rug. Tuck and Teresa were ignoring the fast beat of the music and just slowly grinding against each other. Tuck had his hand on Teresa's ass. Some fat blonde wearing hippie clothes was dancing with my husband. I watched them move together and my husband looked up and saw me and smiled. He motioned for me to come over. I walked over and asked the blonde if I could cut in. She shrugged and spun off, dancing by herself, twirling around and around.

I danced with my husband. Then the guy with the walrus mustache asked me to dance. So I danced with him. He told me I smelled good. Then I danced a slow dance with a little gay guy named Jose while his lover Johno looked on and called him a slut.

"What a wonderful dancer you are, Mami," said Jose. "So light on your feet."

After that, I danced with Chad who only had an arm and a half. He clapped his hand to his stump to keep time.

In between partners, I danced by myself.

I danced with anyone who wanted me to but it wasn't

making me feel any better. So finally I stopped and sat down on a pink velvet chair.

My husband handed me a glass of red wine. "How do you feel?" he asked.

I sipped the wine. "This place..." I said, "I can't stand thinking about what Tuck's going to do to it."

"I know," said my husband.

"It's a crime," I said.

"I know," said my husband.

"It should be us," I whispered.

"I know," said my husband. He drank some of my wine. He cupped his hand to my cheek. He bent and pushed his forehead against mine. "Let's go upstairs," he said.

I tried to take him up to the solarium, but he was moving too fast. He was touching my hair and running his hands down my back and over my hips. We got to the second floor and he took my hand and pulled me into a room. It was the library. Floor to ceiling bookshelves with hundreds of leather-bound books and white brocade chairs and couches scattered across a dark wood floor.

"Look," I said.

My husband tugged me down onto the couch.

"Wait," I said. "Look. Look around." I took a sip of wine.

My husband shook his head and reached for my hand.

"Wait," I said.

The glass flew out of my hand. The wine splattered across the back of the couch and dripped down in a pool on the seat. I stared at the deep purple red stain that was seeping into the brocaded roses.

I couldn't breathe.

Kate Schapira

)) ———————————————————————

Steal From Me

The burglars hit their third house last week. The Hertwilers came home from their daughter's in East Windsor and found the glass in the front door smashed. Mr. Hertwiler cut his wrist and hand trying to open it. He sent his wife next door to call the police and the Willises' Doberman almost bit her. Mr. Hertwiler said later that they'd thought they were safe because of that damn dog but it couldn't even do the one thing you'd think it'd be good for, that is to say scaring the pants off people. The Doberman could have barked itself deaf and the Willises—along with everyone else within hearing—would have adjusted their earplugs and gone back to sleep.

It was a change for the burglars. The other two houses had been out on back roads where nobody went, except people who live there and drivers looking for a shortcut they would never find. Bigger houses. Houses with children, two cars, more to lose.

Yesterday Mimi found a dead snake, run over and then frozen, on the side of the road. She brought it inside and hid it in her sister's bed. Jay says his children are devil's changelings and he's not feeding them anymore. He pours milk into a saucepan, turns the heat on low, adds sugar from a pottery jar and baker's cocoa from a tin can. "The trick is to keep stirring," he says to Jonas, his eldest, tall for his age and thin with big eyes in a big head. Jonas nods and stirs vigorously. Jay says, "Okay, buddy, lemme do this part," and pours, filling each mug halfway, then topping off with what's left. All three children watch him with eyes like mugs of cocoa. One for Mimi. One for Jonas. One for Lily. One for Jay. And one for me.

A pattern begins to appear. The burglars prefer houses with one story, and what they can't carry, they break. TV screens hammered in. Dishes apparently thrown into the air before smashing on linoleum. They slash couch cushions and shit on the carpet. Anything small—cash, jewelry, bankbooks, in one house Nintendo games—disappears. The Marshes' car was set on fire.

This township started out a burglar's dream. Nobody locked the doors to house or car. Now I even lock the high-up bathroom window before I leave for work. I wonder why the burglars are setting themselves up this way. If they just took the small things without wreaking havoc, it might be a while before anyone noticed their valuables' absence, but each destruction worsens their chances of finding easy prey. They must hate us so much.

We've had a hard freeze. Out for my walk I pass Nancy Barron down in the culvert with Ruthie, her two-year-old. Ruthie teeters on the double-bladed skates strapped to her puffy snowboots. Nancy holds her up and yells to me, "The ice is three inches thick!"

"That's great!" I call back. The pools created by the culvert, on either side of our road, are about ten feet in diameter, busy with frogs in the summertime. Nancy says, "Wave, honey." Ruthie waves. She looks like Miss Korean America, a sober child with a little dish of a face and an intense regard, now directed toward her feet. "Push, glide," Nancy says to her. Skating is one of the things you can do around here in the winter. To ski you have to drive at least an hour. Lots of people do it anyway who can afford it.

Nancy quit her job at the bank when Ruthie came to her and her husband Todd. Her hips and belly spread and softened as if she had really been pregnant with Ruthie and brought her to birth. There were plenty of unkind comments in the velvet-roped line at the bank. The skin of Nancy's face always looks a little tight and shiny, which makes me uncomfortable, but I love to watch her with her daughter. For Dr. Barron I have no use whatsoever. When he looks at you it's like being stalked by a reptile and his clothes are always spotless.

The police issue a statement about what to do, what not to do if you come home while the burglars are still there. This hasn't happened yet—the crimes are usually at least a few hours old, the turds on the rug beginning to cool and dry, by the time they're discovered—but it's everyone's fear. The local paper prints the list, bordered in black, on page three. We are good at being told what not to do.

The Barrons install a burglar alarm. Mrs. Hertwiler tells me that she and her husband are thinking of moving to East Windsor, to be near their daughter and her family, and Mr. Chotiros, whose house hasn't been touched but who lives out on Kominsky Lane not far from the Barrons and me, sleeps with his Korean War pistol next to his bed.

The ground is almost too hard to walk on. It's been a dry winter. One of the burglars leaves a size thirteen print in the frost outside the Horvaths' screen porch.

Jay says, "Tricia called yesterday."

She hasn't called him in two months, I know. When my sister talks to me we don't mention Jay at all. "What'd she say?"

"She said did I want her to take the kids for awhile."

"Because of the burglaries." He nods. "You don't have to let her."

"I know," he says.   Lily comes into the kitchen and nuzzles her father's knee. This is usually a prelude to asking for something. He flexes his big hand on her downy head, pretending to suck her brain. It's too much for me; I get up and go into the "big room," which is living room, Jay's bedroom, kids' playroom, the room where we used to push back the couches and dance. A pot of water on top of the woodstove, stained with old overflows, battles the dry air with steam. The kids want snow. I stand by the window and look out at their unkempt backyard, the empty rabbit hutch that the kids plead every year to populate, a forlorn plastic sled like a beetle shell.

Two weeks go by without any reports of shadowy intruders or strange night noises. Everyone relaxes. Moonlight snowball fights resume. The drugstore puts up its Valentine's Day decorations and fills its shelves with heart-shaped boxes, white teddy bears that jingle when you squeeze their feet.

On the night of February third Anna Kominsky comes home to find her house trashed and has a heart attack. Mikey Lucker, who gardens for her and has a house on the premises, finds her and drives her to Vassar Brothers. She may make it. I can't bring myself to ask Dr. Todd. I know somebody will tell me soon.

She was the ideal victim, an old woman living alone with her bad heart. Mikey is out at the bar most nights, only antibiotics kept him home that evening. Why did they wait so long? We all want to understand them. What about our lives says, Steal from me?

Every time I come home I try to prepare myself, especially since it's dark when I get done with work. I'll find shit smears on my beloved red couch, my paintings slashed to streamers, footprints in spilled flour and sugar, the emergency fund gone from my mother's old shoebag. Winter will come in through the broken glass. And then where will I go? To my mother and Richard in North Carolina? Not to Tricia. Even if I wanted to live in New York, even if she and Serge would take me in, I could never live with her now. Twelve years sharing a room was more than enough. It was strange for her to express concern, out of character, but they're her kids too.

Jay doesn't own a washer or a dryer. He, or sometimes Jonas, does the family laundry at my house. We strung a clothesline from crabapple to crabapple. In the winter, drying racks clutter my studio till all his clothes smell like turpentine and oil paint. He says one day he'll spontaneously combust when he goes to put wood in the stove. He says it'll be my fault.

Dina Pearlman

———————————————————— ((

The House Goes On Without Us

{photographer ^{2} + ghost = x(house) +y(a)cat}

~a surrealist ghost story~

I.

*G*hosts are flesh turned into houses.

II.

The photographer sleeps.

How does he sleep when the creaks and groans tickle the ear hairs with brush fire tongues? Green cloth stretches beneath his harsh breathing and boxes of faces are stacked up, nestling in the stone corners.

All day, he looks through the world with ground glass and now the world is staring back at him in secret. The night is a blind, slithering beast, working its fingers over his sleeping face. Now he is known.

His mother watches over him, flesh of her flesh, bones of her bones. The city woman sends her familiar to watch the inside of his skull. The four-legged spy looks between the walls for dust couriers, slithering fur past bare legs. The trees are coconspirators

118

also. No one is ever truly alone.

He searches for a cigarette as he awakens. The sulphur glow stings his eyes. How many memories fit on the head of a match? He barely feels the black burn on his resinous fingers.

The other photographer wraps her limbs in the rough, stale blanket, lying awake. Always awake.

He thinks his fidgeting keeps her awake, but it's the cacophonous jazz of red velvet smoking jackets lying cross-armed in waiting upstairs. The upstairs murmurs through her. She is ensconced in these echoes. The quiet exhales stillness into the once shivering trees. Pause.

How could a house be breathing with such jagged breath when it is surrounded with the smooth sighs of lavender, shaggy grass and ever-blooming bushes? He pulls her closer, and she feels the tickle of tendrils against her cheek, the golden fleece carving tiny roads of invasion into her smooth flesh. There are too many molecules to account for.

And it's too difficult, this baseline grid. Only two elements on the Periodic Table can make the difference. Waiting is only part of the equation. The rock is claiming the left side of the house, and makes sleeping hard. In the lonely time of waking, she hears the cat pillow hiss gently as its suggestion slithers to the lighted bathroom.

"Lift your skirts and run, run while you have the chance!"

She remembers the aroma of the low-ceilinged room. She knows that someone inside that upstairs room is waiting to get out. The presence sings in diaphanous strings, lodging between two tomes, fleeting under the eaves, protesting the track lights. It is a she, always a she. She is from that north side rock She is from the gilded eaves She thinks this is different.

"Get out, run," she hears the cries.

Not yet. Tighter. He is the blanket and stops her. It's been done for hundreds of years, and she can't stop it.

III.

She makes him breakfast, sets the table, smells the coffee grinder. The kitchen table is home for dozens of small castles, almost finished meals, oil lamps, coral from the Gulf, more tragic newspapers, cut glass crystal, a single flower and fresh tobacco. It's a dahlia, and it's uncompromising.

Each petal of the flamboyant dahlia sitting crystalline in the minute vase is a finger to the nerve center. The nerves replace the root cellar. They solder even the tiniest hair of desire into night fusion. They convert the thin, wrinkled morning light into long slick waves. They are corporeal soldiers. Dark magenta. A violent dahlia.

Returning from the garden, he offers her a tiny red rose, fragile between two rough fingers of gold. A late Fall rose, demure, submissive under the neighboring dahlia's reign. The redness is sharp citrus and antique sweetness. It rests inside a chipped mauve glass, melancholy in its singleness. The roses were waiting here before.

Upstairs, sighs. Patience.

IV.

Film noir, spangled floors and shadows sprinkling dust. There are too many people in the house, so she touches them all with silent hands. Pedal steel slides into the kitchen from the slate room. Three stained spindly pick-up guitar men dance in old boots and hoot:

"Blow that horn, man, blow it."

Sax and rum have settled inside the crevices, while tobacco fingers snap and all that jazz stuff. Stomping gangly black, jeaned legs to the other generations. Hammond organ. Horns blowing.

Rock on.

"This house is built into the side of a rock, man, built into the side of a rock."

The humming is flat and forthright. It generates chandelier dreams and former cigar smokers wearing crème colored tuxes. Tapping feet, exposed beams. She is exposed and nothing can stop it. She fits her hand under the skin of the wire-knuckled paw of the lanky man.

"Rock, man, rock man,"

There are rooms that no one can get to. There are zones where they do it do it stony and broken. They are books and they play like children. Play that woman, blow that horn, stomp stomp...

"Be bop, be bop,"

They are novellas. They are librettos and sing narcotic ditties. Smoke has laid a claim to the room. She can lose herself into it. Tobacco is the doorway to the other world. Smoke. It is dancing in urgent dervish circles...

"Be bop, be bop pop pop pop, "

Outside the door leading to nowhere. Does any door really do better? She remembers the morning's sun spot confetti of last summer outside the screen, speckled rock inches from the half-tone window. But the memory is lost in the never-ending night.

"Built into the side of a rock, man."

V.

A dim Venus blows bubbles from stained hands. Blue-gold walls steeping dimly yellow reveal the alloted section of intimacy for the raw corners of this house. A sample of this quota. She fits inside the frame like a Chinese box. It never ends. Sweet amber and vanilla float in the oil-slicked waters. Musk is swirling down in the direction of the northern hemisphere. He dips one finger below the surface and applies it to her slickness, causing her to drown for one warm dark pulsating minute.

Unfolded, the closeness is softened by her brine and the four-legged spy cat who leaves hair deposits on her humid legs when she steps out of the bath.

The photographer is lost, sunken. The eyes have it—too many females gaze while he is accordianed into the tiny tub. Only the cat is on his side as he purrs, "*She won't be long for this house. She.*"

By and by, she leaves like a thief. He doesn't notice; it's an irrelevant concept. Affection is just an abstraction... steal away.

VI.

How could night survive its dusky implications?

The sun can't help itself, and it hides in waiting, waiting, waiting till it's physically overcome by the (pregnant) moon. It squashes through the window and is self-absorbed in its fatness. It's not enough force, so reflection is an afterthought. She stares out the window as he takes another picture of her, wearing a dress two hundred years ago. He can't decide between the shutter release or buttons, buttons. He searches her flesh for clues. Too many buttons.

Assisted light from any disk will share the effort. Now the manufactured sun is straining. Desiring to sprinkle daisies inside her mouth as she laughs into the gin-soaked ceiling. She is upstairs. She is getting dusty... when she sneezes old, yellow paper flutters to the floor. Remnants of the old books crack up. She piles them on his cold extremities, and aching rose in quarter note wails till the velvet comfort greenly leveled off. The sound of the house sits damply in the side of a rock. Holding the spine of the book like an interred angel allowed his mother's thumbs to brand a slight gasp from the tissue-thin leaves.

He is surrounded by walls. Each door opens to the next chamber. Somewhere is the heart of it. How many more rooms? The house is larger on the outside. The longer he lives there, the smaller it gets.

Parts of some other centuries reach out and squeeze the core. He is holding out his arm, turreted up high, high. Night terrors tell him that incarceration is willful, that digging out is the wrong route, yet still the female structure strokes his hair with possession when he lies down in the tiny rooms.

It's only safe during the pulsing night. Wings flap wildly when the doors swing open. She offers him dark legs and marbled eyes. He makes the camera open up for the woman. If this one will affix to the silver cells of the film, he will be able to be free. Then he can tell the difference between all the women. One is tactile and seethes, One is inside him, One is lost. One can't get out.

Inside the spoon-filled room, low ceilings are certainly threatening, so why did they stay there? Was it those white fleshy pages? Brittle tight skins? Twice told stories? Plushy damp sages?

Though they had one skin, they couldn't breathe there. Better to recline on brocade pillows while drinking scotch from minute crystal glasses, murmuring in the moldering stew. Why not? It's been done for hundreds of years in this very room.

No one can stop it.

Edward M. Cohen

──────────────────────────────────── ⟨⟨

Arabian Prince

Nothing had ever tasted as good as the greasy cheeseburgers from the All Nite Diner on Strike Nights. They were delivered just as last week's set was coming down and next week's was going up and we were all eager to see the new one erect. Later, when we reached a state of exhaustion bordering on drunkenness, nobody would give a damn. Someone would start on "He's Just My Bill" and we would all hammer along in rhythm until Archie, the designer, would scream that we would never get the fucking flats up with that dreary song in the air. A second wind would come with the dawn and the tune would change to "Anything You Can Do I Can Do Better." Doors would get painted and windows would fly into place. By the time the All Nite Diner delivered breakfast, we could eat in triumph, then get some sleep before dress rehearsal. We were lowly apprentices at the Star Bright Summer Theatre in Middletown, New York and every assignment was thrilling.

I learned to drink my coffee black that summer of '51 because there was no refrigerator in the barn for milk and the only way to get through Strike Nights, and many of the days, was on caffeine. Gigi Dubrow, who had apprenticed at Star Bright the summer before, was teaching me to smoke except that I kept my fingers straight when I held the cigarette so Gigi said I would never learn.

We worked eighteen hours daily; racing from rehearsal to scene shop or out in the company station wagon for props, then back to the theatre at night to usher. One week, my job was to dust the furniture before half-hour. There was an end table on set which was just like one my mother had at home. She must have bought it in the thirties when she got married; dark mahogany with a rim of curlicues, a shelf for magazines, carved legs and little clawed feet.

I had never paid attention to the one at home, much less considered dusting it, but this table looked perfect as part of the overdone hotel suite for "Born Yesterday." That Archie was a genius at detail, I thought, as I sprayed and buffed every corner. After all, the table at home was merely used for my father's nightly newspaper. This table was to be on stage, where everything had to be perfect.

Archie selected every cup, every saucer. There was a lamp shade, stage right, which exactly matched the heroine's dress so that when she entered, stage left, the audience would immediately fall in love, responding to the harmony in the universe. That Archie had everything figured out.

Light cues were set. Furniture was spiked. Archie instructed that a cocktail glass be placed at a specific angle so that Rolf Leslie, the leading man, could pick it up in a comic rhythm and, every night, he lifted it on cue and, every night, it got a laugh. When my parents came to see the show, they said the acting had "seemed so natural," and Gigi and I beamed with condescension.

Even though Gigi was older than I and taller and fatter so everybody snickered, even though we had never necked or even kissed on the lips, I told my parents that we were soul mates and would eventually get married and be the new Lunt and Fontanne of the American theatre and, I silently prayed, everything scary about my life would turn out perfect.

~

One week, Gigi and I were on props and Archie said he pictured the set for "The Tavern" dressed with pewter mugs and plates. Even Gigi did not realize how expensive pewter was, so we spent the day driving around the countryside, knocking on doors, and came back empty-handed; which did not matter because we had gossiped and giggled the whole trip. But Archie exploded. As he howled, I watched Gigi's lips tighten against possible tears and, as usual, followed her lead.

"I didn't say pewter! I said something *like* pewter! Pewter-*ish*! Of course, no one is going to lend you pewter. But this is The Theatre, kiddies, not real life. If the blue-haired ladies won't lend you pewter, you get aluminum and spray! You do not waste the entire day and tie up the company wagon circling the highways and byways of Middletown, looking for fucking pewter!"

"But you said pewter," Gigi insisted.

"Oh Gigi, grow up! You're not a virgin anymore. You're supposed to be a professional by now. I can understand little Kenny making dum-dum mistakes like this. But you, Gigi, you should know better!"

He stormed off to his drawing board and Gigi ran into the ladies' room to cry. Archie always turned up his radio when he got angry so we each had grown attached to tunes: Rosemary Clooney's "Come On-A My House," Eddie Fisher's "Oh, My Papa." As if on cue, my favorite, Tony Bennett's "Because of You" floated through the cool basement that served as scene shop, a sure sign that things would work out.

After all, Archie wasn't mad at me, so I waited to see if he would look up and smile, maybe bark what he wished me to do next, but he was hunched over his charcoal pencil, pouring his rage into next week's design—"A Streetcar Named Desire"— which, Gigi said, was going to be his masterpiece.

If anyone else had called me "Little Kenny"—say any of the dum-dum guys in my dum-dum neighborhood, who were spending their summers doing dum-dum things like working as camp counselors—I would have been insulted, but Archie and I were theatre pros, not virgins. Except, of course, that I was.

I was reminded because, this time, I sensed that there was no reason to follow Gigi by running off to cry. Something in the way Archie had called me "Little Kenny" was strangely reassuring. So I lit up a Pall Mall with curled fingers and awaited further instruction.

~

On opening night of "The Tavern," Gigi, looking weird in her usher's outfit of a dress and high heels, and I, uncomfortable in white shirt and tie, stood at the back of the house and embraced as the set, littered with sprayed aluminum, received a round of applause.

The show went smoothly, even though Monte Hammond, the character man, had his lines hidden on scraps of paper all over the furniture. Nobody in the audience seemed to notice, and we all went out afterwards to celebrate at the Log Cabin Tavern. The next day we were off, and Gigi and I were going into town to see Mario Lanza in "The Great Caruso." The day after was the first read-through of "Streetcar."

Gigi said we were fickle whores. While we were playing one show at night, we were flirting with the next. By the time last week's was ready to close, we were already screwing with the new and, as soon as it had opened, we were getting the hots for the one coming up.

Gigi always talked about screwing on opening nights. When we were hunting for props, the years between us—she was eighteen, I was fifteen—did not matter but, at the Log Cabin Tavern, where she could drink and I could not, she turned into a creature from another planet; running after all the guys, dancing alone when no one would have her.

The others laughed and prodded her on, but I was the one who had to get her home, wake her in the morning, pump her up with coffee, describe what she had done and hold her hand while she wept in mortification.

"Was Archie there when I danced with my skirt above my head?"

"I'm afraid so, Gigi."

"All summer, I haven't worn shorts, no matter how hot it was, just so he shouldn't see my despicable thighs!"

"Well, they were playing 'Hernando's Hideaway.' That's your favorite tune."

"It's ruined for me for eternity."

"Another thing you did, that you shouldn't have, is you threw your arms around him."

"Oh no! I didn't!"

"You know how Archie hates to be touched."

"What did he do?"

"He screamed and ran away which everyone thought was a laugh riot."

"Poor Archie..."

"Poor Gigi..."

"How he must hate me!"

"Matter of fact, he helped get you home. He drove us in the company wagon."

"If I've screwed up his design for 'Streetcar,' I'll never forgive myself!"

"Don't you remember anything that happened?"

"He's so sensitive. He's a great artist. How am I ever going to make it up to him?"

"Poor Gigi..."

"Poor Archie..."

~

Nobody knew what was wrong with Archie, with his phobias and moodiness and tantrums, but clearly something was. At times, he could be giddy and charming but there was always the danger of an explosion. Which is why I should have been more suspicious when he came up to me at the Log Cabin Tavern and whispered that we had to get Gigi out of there; the way she was spinning around the dance floor, she was sure to pass out any minute. We both approached and slid our arms under her twirling elbows and lifted her off her feet and carried her to the door while the rest of the company laughed and applauded and we pretended it was part of the gag.

When we got to the parking lot we dumped her in the back of the wagon and she seemed to fall asleep the minute her head hit the seat. After all that noise and tumult, Archie lit a cigarette and offered me one and I sucked on the flame from his lighter.

The jukebox barely hummed in the distance. There were no cars coming or going. The only sound was that of my pounding heart. I looked into Archie's eyes to see if he could hear it and, the way he looked back, I knew that he could.

But this was 1951 and I suddenly understood, from the sweat on his brow, that he was more scared than I was.

~

Gigi wept all through "The Great Caruso," but I guessed that it was not because of the movie. Sure enough, she announced afterwards that Mario Lanza was an utter no-talent, but the boredom had given her time to do a thorough self-analysis.

"I want to explain something to you, Kenny, something I haven't mentioned before because I didn't want to disillusion you."

"Gigi, you can tell me anything. I was there when it happened."

"What are you talking about?"

"What are *you* talking about?"

"I'm talking about the fact that every show we have done so far has been worthless. 'The Moon Is Blue,' 'Born Yesterday,' 'The Tavern;' commercial claptrap programmed for the bourgeoisie!"

"Oh Gigi, don't put everything down just because you're hung over."

"Sometimes I am actually jealous because I can no longer view life with your adolescent naiveté."

129

"Marcella is a brilliant director! Rolf Leslie has star quality! Archie is a genius! You've said so yourself!"

"But the plays, my darling, are pure crap and the self-deception is what causes me to crack up on opening nights like Zelda Fitzgerald."

"Gigi, you do not crack up. You just drink too much and do stupid things like dance with your skirt around your head!"

"Oh, shut up about that!"

~

Archie took off with a furious screech, but in the wrong direction; not toward town but away from it, not via the main road but through dark woods filled with baying dogs.

"Where are you going?" I cried.

"Taking a short cut."

"Archie! You're going to get lost!"

"Shut your trap, faggot!"

I stared at him in disbelief.

"I'm going be sick!" Gigi moaned from the back.

A moment ago, I had felt desire tingling up my thighs. Now, paralysis was numbing my senses. A moment ago, we seemed to be heading toward perfection. "The Tavern" had opened and "Streetcar" was next. Now, we were bouncing along dirt roads while Gigi, in a panic, attempted to raise herself by grabbing Archie's hair from behind, which forced him to jam on the brakes so we were all thrown forward and she nearly tumbled into the front seat.

"Gigi! Are you all right?"

"Didn't I tell you to shut up?" Archie sneered. "I'll take care of her."

Gigi opened the back door and her limp body fell onto the grass with a thump. We immediately heard her throwing up.

"We'll see about this lousy cunt who wants to grope me all over so everybody howls and then she thinks she can puke all over the company wagon. I've been taken by smarter than this loud-mouthed bitch so she'd better be ready to pay and here's the coin of the realm!"

He reached into his pocket for a thin rubber disc packaged in tinfoil and held it up for me to see. I knew what it was. Eli Wallach's character had dropped one on stage in "The Rose Tattoo," causing a flurry of Letters to the Editor of the Sunday Times Theatre Section. Every hood on my dum-dum block had one rotting in his wallet, but it had never occurred to me that Archie did too. It did occur to me that he was putting on this show for me.

He lumbered from the wagon and lifted Gigi, as casually as he had lifted a window frame during Strike Night for "The Tavern." I called as he carried her off into the dark but my voice trailed limply behind him.

What else was I supposed to do? Scream for help in the middle of the woods? Follow after and wrestle him off her? Crash back into the Log Cabin Tavern, as if I could ever find it in the dark, screaming "RAPE!" over the strains of "The Tennessee Waltz?" Would anyone believe me? Would anyone care?

The wagon door had been left swinging on its hinges, squeaking repeatedly, and the glaring overhead bulb revealed a copy of Variety on the seat beside me. Quickly I reached for it and buried my nose into news of which shows were doing boffo business and which ones were not, but the light attracted too many bugs so I shut the door, which offered the advantage of preventing me from hearing Gigi screaming, just in case she was.

~

Usually, after a movie, Gigi dissected each scene like a French film critic, and she applied the same judgmental talent to her life, her emotions, her art. After "The Great Caruso," we bought vanilla cones with chocolate sprinkles and sat on a bench outside the drug store, watching the sun set in a cloudless sky.

This week would be different from all the others, Gigi explained, because "A Streetcar Named Desire" was, at last, a work worthy of our talents. Marcella Rae South, Star Bright's founder, was taking an artistic flyer by scheduling it and this was our chance to pave the way for serious drama in upstate New York.

Sure, Jessica Tandy and Marlon Brando had been brilliant on Broadway but, when it came time to bring art to the townies, it fell to the likes of us: Marcella, who would be playing Blanche as well as directing, Rolf as Stanley.

And Archie, Gigi said, had simply outdone himself. She had seen his sketches and he was creating the entire back wall out of window shutters—"very New Orleans," she declared, her voice assuming a Southern lilt although she was only assigned to costumes.

Scenes could be played with the shutters open or shut so that, as the curtain rises, the audience would see Blanche wandering upstage, looking for the proper address.

"They tol' me to take a streetcar named Desire," Gigi drawled.

And, at the end, after she has been raped by Stanley, when she leaves on the arm of a doctor—"Ah have always depended on the kahndness of strangers"—she would be fading off in a long, tragic, beautiful exit.

I was lucky to have a small part as The Young Collector and Gigi said I had a crucial scene in which I got kissed and Blanche uttered one of the play's famous lines: "Young, young, young, young...man! Has anyone ever told you that you look like a young prince out of the Arabian Nights?"

"Isn't that pure poetry, Kenny?"

In Tennessee Williams, Gigi said, everything was poetic: suicide, madness, rape; even faggotry, because Blanche is haunted by the memory of her secretly queer husband who was so ashamed that he blew his brains out behind the Moon Lake Casino while she was dancing the Varsouviana, and every time she thinks of him it's a cue for exquisite background music.

~

Almost immediately it seemed, certainly sooner than I had expected, Archie returned to the wagon; shoulders slumped, back curled, head drooping. Gigi followed, her eyes—shining dark marbles when she was happy—tightened into suspicious slits. This time, she tossed herself into the back, whistling "Hernando's Hideaway" as bugs invaded and circled the bulb.

Nothing could have happened, I thought, not that quickly. Not that I knew how much time it would have taken to have happened. Anyway, I knew that whatever was supposed to have happened hadn't happened because Archie laid his head against the steering wheel and wept.

"I didn't," he sighed. "…I couldn't…" and then and there I knew I would have him and Gigi would end up hating us both.

~

That sunset, after "The Great Caruso," Gigi threw an arm around my shoulders as if she were the boy and I the girl and announced that on the opening night of "Streetcar" she would have no need to use alcohol to numb her self-hatred because we were doing such hack work. Instead, she would be proud of me, of Archie, of the entire company, of the glory of The Theatre. And we had seen the coming attractions of next week's feature: Ava Gardner, Howard Keel, Kathryn Grayson in "Show Boat."

"After 'Streetcar' is a smash and we have an opening night party at which I do not touch a drop—and I finally get my hands on Archie—you and I are going to see 'Show Boat' and we'll cry our eyes out. Right, Kenny? Oh God, I love him so!"

"Listen, Gigi. I've got to tell you what happened!"

"When?"

"Last night."

"What?"

"He said he was going to rape you!"

"Who?"

"Archie!"

To my surprise, she doubled over with laughter.

"Oh, honey chile, every time a fella gets mad at his gal, he says he's gawna rape her!"

I was so stunned that I giggled along with her. Also because I was the one who now had everything figured out.

"And what did you do, mah Arabian Prince? Jump out and save me?"

I could not tell her what had actually happened; I was too ashamed. I could not tell her how I planned to finally get my hands on Archie. She would have been too shocked. Instead, I nestled my head in her shoulder so we could sing those lines together—"Young, young, young, young...man!"—bursting into raucous laughter as passing townies stared.

)) ——————————————————————————

Electricity

Señor."

"The old man caught the corner of my eye as I left the sidewalk behind him to cross the narrow street.

"Señor," he repeated, a little louder this time. I stopped in the middle of the quiet lane and turned toward him.

"Señor—do you speak Spanish?" The old man's voice was not as fragile as it first appeared. The slight Hispanic lilt gave his midrange tenor an air of formality that most Americans find, frankly, a bit uncomfortable.

I'd noticed him from a hundred feet or so, his pale straw fedora and open-side poncho hard to miss in the tranquil, upstate surroundings of the hospital grounds. He walked with a cane, the kind with a t-shaped bone handle and a dark hardwood shaft. It was old—he'd had it for quite a while. As I'd gained on him, a thought sprang from the ether: *This is how you'll look. This could be—will be—you, someday. Not too far off, either.*

He was in no hurry, and I'd come nearly abreast of him when I'd detoured to cross the street on my way to a lunch date. He turned fully toward me now as I stood in the road, his long hair and beard corkscrewing around his face, a loose white frame. The serious look told me he was a man who believed in what he was about to say.

"No, I do not," I told him evenly. I knew there was more.

"I am over one hundred years old," he began, and counted on his five fingers as he held up a knotty, weathered hand. "Five months ago. January. I celebrated my one hundredth birthday in

January."

He watched me as I smiled. "That's wonderful," I told him, not wanting to seem to be uninterested in his longevity accomplishments. In truth, it surprised me – he looked maybe late seventies, early eighties to me. What do I know?

"Forty doctors," he continued. "I worked at the hospital for fifteen years, with forty doctors. I am left. Not one of them. Only me. One hundred years old. And I say that what you are doing," he paused for effect, "is wrong. It is bad for you."

I was nonplussed. "What?"

"There is electricity," he said, not to be interrupted. "Everywhere. Our bodies run on electricity. The ground. The air. Everywhere. You disrupt the flow, doing what you do."

"I'm confused," and, genuinely, I was. Electricity?

"How old are you?" he asked.

"Forty-one," I replied, and smiled again. People always told me I look young for my age. People probably told him that, too. He grunted.

"This Viagra. This sex drug. Grown men, thirties, forty years old. They need this Viagra. They can't get the erection no more. Why?" He was way past me now, but I was fascinated. How is he going to tie *this* all back together?

"Because they do like you. They interrupt the electricity. It flows up the left side of your body. Swirls around. Down the right side. It comes from the ground. Your body needs it. You must not do that anymore," he finished, nodding solemnly.

"Do what? What am I doing?"

"This!" he shouted as he thrust his hands into the pockets at the front of his pants.

The old man must have seen the confusion still written in my expression, because he offered more.

"This," he said more calmly as he shook his hands in the pockets of his loose linen pants, "interrupts the flow. The electricity? Nowhere to go. It is bad for you. The electricity needs to reach out." He removed his hands from his pockets.

"You need to be grounded. We all need to be grounded."

Until that moment, I hadn't realized I'd even had my hands in my pockets. I looked at his brown eyes. They seemed part of the younger look of the man, even buried as they were among the wrinkles of a sun-weathered face. He wasn't kidding.

I took my hands out of my pockets. The man smiled.

"I am a Mayan Indian," he said. "My people know about these things. We have known about the electricity for hundreds of years. We are strong people. The electricity makes us strong. And so I outlive all the doctors. All of them. They walked like you do, hands in their pants. They stopped the flow.

"It is the best thing you can do. Let the electricity flow. In the winter, do you know what I do? I wear gloves. It's OK. But I never put my hand in my pocket unless I need to get something out. In, out. That's OK. What you were doing," he pointed a crooked finger at my hips, "is not."

"Thank you," I said. "I didn't know that such a thing was bad for me. I will consider your advice."

"You keep your hands free. The electricity will swirl," he demonstrated as he moved his hand in circles around his chest, "And you no have problems like those Viagra men. You get the erection."

He turned to continue his walk, then turned back.

"Remember," he said, "Remember the electricity. You have a good day."

He walked away at his snail's pace down the sidewalk as I finished crossing the road, my own gait slower, my gaze more thoughtful. I could smell the blossoms of an apple tree as I passed it, their white petals in bloom for just these few days. Maybe he was mad—this was a psychiatric hospital, after all. He might have been just another patient.

Or maybe he was a one hundred year old Mayan. My hands swung freely as I headed for lunch.

Ty Adams

ᚓᚓ

The Chain Thief

~To Rudy "Red" Manley, who taught me how to whistle.~

At first light, my eyes begin fluttering. A daily pleasure. The air in my cell is thick with the smell of bacon and biscuits. Make any eye flutter, bacon and biscuits. Y'see, my cell is the last one on the corridor. Next to the kitchen. So I get the good stuff, first thing in the morning.

But to get to the morning, I have to sleep safe, and to keep safe when I sleep, I make myself the size of a baby's fingernail. I figure, no baby's ever woke up missin' a fingernail.

The sudden sound of a guard's stick rattling across my cell bars brings me up and sittin'.

–Rise and shine, Rudy.

–Yessir.

–Sheriff Cody's birthday.

–Yessir.

–Rise and shine, boy.

–Yessir.

–I wantcha to take this broom and dust rag over to the gym; clean it good; ya got three hours.

–Yessir.

–Big day today for Sheriff Cody.

–Yessir.

And so it began. Sheriff Cody's... Big Day. I cleared my eyes and let my imagination play. I figured, back in the time of King Arthur; him returnin' to the castle after a long war; everybody was told to grab somethin', clean somethin' and clean it good and make everythin' juuust right.

So I twisted the ole blue dust rag juuust right, into a face shape, tossed it to my shoulder to rest, facin' forward like a new friend takin' a ride.

—Let's go get this big day!

I made my way down the corridor, past the kitchen; there'd be no breakfast for me this morning; past the sound of newspaper wrinklin'; past the smell of fresh coffee; past Jabbo Stokes's radio blastin'; past the main-man; through the gate and across the concrete exercise yard, to the gymnasium.

There was no way I could've known that this day would be any different. I never made plans. I just lived day-to-day; but as the cobwebs cleared my eyes, I sensed a feelin'... a feelin' I had gotten up with; a feelin' that happened when the guard woke me; a fleetin' glimpse of a feelin' passed over me when the sound of that stick moved past my cell, rattlin' in the air. Maybe I wasn't quick enough to remember this feelin' clearly, but it happened; it lived inside me and right now a voice in me was tellin' me that this day, Sheriff Cody's birthday, Cody's Big Day... would be my last.

The gym was filled with foldin' metal chairs donated by the Southern Yacht Club of New Orleans. Proud members donated money and got their names spelled out in gold on the back of the chairs. This was to tell future generations who was generous and who wasn't. I found this amusin' 'cause I knew the difference between real gold and gold paint from the prison fix-it shop. There's a difference between fake and real... future generations will not be fooled.

I stared at the backside of the chairs. All them names, important peoples' names starin' at me. I was sent here to clean 'em. I felt bad about that. What kinda job was that for a man? 'Specially a black man? Cleanin' names on the back of chairs. Then I looked to my right shoulder, and a blue dust rag face of a new friend gave me an idea....

—We'll dust these chairs with the names, last.

139

I strutted off feelin' good. Me and my little dust rag friend had obtained some unauthorized power. I would make these chairs with the names, wait.

I strutted myself to the front, hopped up on the stage. Sat on the edge, facin' the chairs. Sheriff Cody had his mind right when he ordered this gym built with a stage. Thinkin' entertainment for the inmates. Only now, lookin' down on the chairs, I didn't feel like a inmate. Lookin' down on the chairs, I felt like a storyteller.

This'll be the spot. I'll put some tape down here. The microphone'll be about... here. And on the front row, all the politicians, the mayor of New Orleans, the governor, my boss the prison warden, all their wives, and the rows behind 'em, the rest of the prison population. But *this chair*, right here on the stage... this is Sheriff Cody's chair. The guest of honor. Sixty-fifth birthday. The man who's done more for prisoners in the State of Louisiana than any other. The prisoner's best friend, Sheriff Cody, right here.

Y'see, thirty years ago, he was a young man, the youngest sheriff ever elected in Orleans Parish. Here's what he did: he, he went out and got money from the politicians and built this gymnasium; started a prisoner's boxin' program, respected nationwide; he, he, he got more books for the prison library than any other sheriff before 'im; and he got businesses around the state to network and hire ex-cons... that's big; give an ex-con a job 'cause Sheriff Cody's word was behind that ex-con. Business people believed him; and that's why we are gatherin' here today at a prison gymnasium to celebrate this man who has done so much for the downtrodden.

But that's not the man I know; y'see, my relationship with Sheriff Cody goes back, way back....

When he was elected Sheriff, I was a little boy; couldn't've been mo' than six years old; I used to tap dance for pennies on the street in the French Quarter; my papa worked on the river durin' the day; we were a team, my papa and me... a tap dancin' duet. I'd time it just right every day to be by the house when he'd come home from the docks; he was more tired than anything I'd ever seen; workin' on the Mississippi was dangerous, hard work but he loved his work and he loved that river; said that river was his best friend. That's why I couldn't understand at the time....

It was a Sunday, late, and I was waitin' for papa to come home; he was later than usual, I could tell by the sun, the way it usually hit the roof across the street and cast a shade on me just 'bout the time he got home every day; only this day I'd been in the shade 'bout an hour when this dark car drives up and Sheriff Cody gets out; sounded real nice...

—Come along boy, yo papa wants to see ya.

Now Papa always told me not to fight with white people so I got in the car; we musta drove across the river down one of them long levy dirt roads; all I remember is lookin' out the back window at the dust flyin' up and nobody sayin' nothin'... just smokin' cigars. All of a sudden, we stop. One of 'em picks me up and I can see flashlights down by the river; figured my papa's probably down there; we walk down and I'm walkin' beside the sheriff but I don't see papa; somebody says...

—Bring him over here.

Now I hadn't been scared up 'til then, when my whole face peeled off in chill after chill...there was my papa; all wrapped up in heavy chains and they're pullin' him outa the river; I knew he was gone and I was glad those nice white men was helpin' me get him out; Sheriff Cody kneeled down beside me...

—This yo papa boy?

—Yes sir.

—Whadaya reckon he wanted to try an' swim the river for?

—I don't know, sir.

—Whadaya reckon he wanted to steal that chain for?

—I don't know, sir.

—Any you boys know why these nigger-chain-thieves wanta keep tryin' to swim this dangerous river? Beats the hell outa me.

And I kept thinkin', that river was his friend; it wouldn't do that to him, no it wouldn't.

So we're gonna put the microphone about... here. And as Sheriff Cody figures... the prisoners will come out one at a time and play their music; we got some good musicians here, and me, I'm suppose to tap dance. Sheriff Cody has said he's seen me dance and knows I'm a good hoofer and he knows I'll do my best. But I was never the hoofer my papa was... no, I see myself as a storyteller, and the microphone'll be about here.

)) ————————————————————————————

Paradise Night Shift

It was mid-November but the afternoon Florida sun shone warmly in a cloudless blue sky. The slight but steady breeze blowing across Clearwater Bay was just cool enough to make the difference between an uncomfortably hot day and a glorious one.

The weather suited Harry Parker's mood. He stepped back, paintbrush in hand, and admired his work. The twenty-four foot sloop, *Isabella*, had arrived at the boatyard a mess. The topsides had been painted a vile green, and were cracked and peeling in places and scarred from banging and rubbing against docks. Apparently the former owner had cared little for the boat and it made Harry angry. The boat was old, but soundly and lovingly built and deserved better treatment.

Happily, her new owner agreed and could afford to remedy the situation. Much of the rigging had been replaced, all the teak had been stripped and re-varnished, the bottom had been scraped, sanded, and given a new coat of anti-fouling paint, and now Harry indulged in a satisfied grin as he examined his own contribution. It had taken an awful lot of sanding, four coats of primer and three coats of paint, but now the white hull gleamed proudly in the sunshine, sleek and with that deep luster that cannot be matched by fiberglass, even at its newest.

He picked up the can in which he had mixed his personal formula of paint, turpentine, and linseed oil and headed for the tiny corrugated shack where the yard workers kept their tools and cleaned up. It was four-thirty, too late to begin working on another job. He would take his time cleaning up. Laughter reached him as he approached the shack. Apparently the others had knocked off even earlier.

Harry stepped through the door and stopped for a moment to allow his eyes to become accustomed to the dimly lit interior after the brilliant sunshine.

"Holy shit, would you look at that?" said a voice Harry recognized as Hobie Turner's. "Parker's got more goddamn paint on him than he put on the boat! They're gonna have to give that owner a fifty percent discount on the job."

Harry smiled and made his way to the little wooden cupboard where he kept his brushes and tools. Hobie was the yard's self-appointed jester.

"You know, Harry," Hobie continued, "instead of scrubbin' off what you've got on you, you ought to slop a little more on, cover up the fleshy spots. Be a damned sight easier."

The others laughed at this ribbing and Harry joined in. He glanced at himself in the tiny cracked and paint-spattered mirror above the sink. His face was covered with white specks.

"I never claimed to be neat," he said.

"And don't never do so," chimed in Billy Duncan in his Tennessee drawl. He was in his late teens and new to the yard and trying hard to fit in. "Elseways you goin' straight to the devil with no shoes and socks on!" he added, grinning happily as everyone laughed.

"Now what in ever-lovin' blue-eyed heaven does that mean?" asked Hobie, seizing on this new target. "No socks on? What the hell's the difference what you're wearin' in a situation like that? How you plannin' to go, Billy? Formal? Devil don't — and this will come as welcome news to you, Brother Parker,—devil don't give no points for neatness. Fact is lack of footwear might be just the thing down there in the tropics. Swimmin' suit's maybe what you need. Don't you agree, Brother Parker?"

"Amen, Brother Turner. Amen," Harry said. He dipped his paint-covered hands and arms into the oil drum filled with acetone that stood beside the sink and scrubbed them.

"But what about your feet?" Billy asked. "They'd burn up on the coals."

Harry couldn't tell whether Billy was joking or seriously concerned.

Hobie patted Billy on the shoulder. "Ah, you poor, confused, ignorant son of a bitch. Just proves what I've always said. Tennessee does produce the ignorantest breed of sinners the good Lord has to bear with. But it's their saving grace. Your ignorance shall be your salvation, Brother Duncan. The ignorant shall inherit something, but they won't know what it is.

"Now, on the other hand, take Brother Parker here. He's an educated man. A college man. And from the big city, too. He knows things. Thinks things. Things that would make that little Bible Belt brain of yours melt with fright if he told them to you.

"Nothin's gonna save Brother Parker," Hobie said. "He can't do nothin' wrong without knowin' it's so. And believe me, Billy, that man's done plenty wrong. Otherwise, what's he doin' here? Did you ever think about that, Billy? What's this yankee college man doin' here makin' three dollars an hour and up to his elbows in acetone? I'll tell you what he's doin', Billy. He's hidin' out. Hidin' out. But there's one thing he don't know, Billy. He don't know that you can't hide from the devil. We know that though, don't we, Billy? You can't hide from the dark one. The devil always gets his due. But Brother Parker don't know that. He can't know that. 'Cause if he did, he'd be shakin' so constant that every waterline he cut in with that brush of his would look like the Rocky Mountains. So he can't know, can he, Billy?"

Billy, wide-eyed and mesmerized by Hobie's patter, slowly shook his head.

"Unless, of course," Hobie added in a stage whisper, putting his hand on the boy's shoulder and leaving it there, "unless he *is* Satan." He slapped Billy's back and laughed loudly. "Think about it, boy! Quittin' time!" he shouted after a glance at the clock on the wall. "Come along, Brother Duncan, let's wander on over to the great time clock of life and punch out."

Hobie and Billy left, followed by the rest of the yard crew except for Harry, who had not finished cleaning his brush, and Jim Hanson, who was rearranging the contents of his locker. Jim was in his early thirties, only a few years older than Harry, but the deeply tanned face beneath his close-cropped dark hair was creased and leathery from too much sun and too many cigarettes. During Harry's nine months at the yard, Jim had taught him everything about painting boats—a far more complicated business than most people realize. They often worked together on bigger jobs and had become close friends. Harry was a frequent dinner guest at the Hansons'. Jim's wife Nora had been waging an unsuccessful but unceasing campaign to get Harry married—or at least firmly attached—since the night she had met him. So far, her efforts had succeeded only in providing Jim and Harry with a lot to laugh about.

"Hobie shouldn't get on that kid like that," Jim said when the others had gone.

"Probably keep him awake nights," Harry said.

~

It was a beautiful evening for the yard's monthly fish-fry and after showering and changing clothes Harry decided to walk the two miles back from his apartment. The breeze had become a whisper, enough to rustle the leaves overhead but no more. He strolled along the road bordering the bay and watched the sun slide toward the horizon. Smoke rose in the distance from the boatyard and he pictured the charcoal fire that would be set up outside the office. The walk had sharpened his appetite. His stomach growled and he smiled as he quickened his pace.

The first person Harry noticed was Nora Hanson. Her brilliant blond hair stood out among the heads of the other women like a beacon. Instantly Harry saw the flashing reflection of Karen's hair beside her. The daughter was a miniature of the mother—slender, gracefully proportioned, straight hair clipped tightly behind the head. Nora stirred a great pot of what Harry suspected was beans and molasses on one of the outdoor gas stoves. It was one of her specialties and one of his favorites. Karen peered eagerly over the rim of the pot, straining on her tiptoes for every inch of height.

Cynthia Collins, daughter-in-law of the boatyard's owner Jake Collins, tended a steaming cauldron of chowder while her husband, Jake Jr.—"Junior" to everyone who knew him—had charge of the deep-fryer, with the enthusiastic assistance of Billy Duncan.

Jake had reserved the best job for himself, cooking oysters over the charcoal fire until they opened and passing them out to be eaten with lemon and hot sauce. Not much work and lots of time for conversation and sipping at a nearby glass of bourbon which seemed somehow never to be less than half full. Jake had been a boatbuilder for over forty years and was a legend in the business. He was tough and determined, but this was tempered with kindness and an understanding of people that inspired deep loyalty and fondness in his employees.

Several women busily arranged bowls of potato salad and coleslaw and piles of plates and utensils on a long table. The men mostly gathered around the charcoal grill—in part because Jake was a notably witty conversationalist, and in part because the bar had been set up on a table there.

Everyone was intent on their business and Harry's arrival was barely noticed, although he did get a smile and a wave from Nora and Karen. He spotted Jim seated at a picnic table, glass in one hand. Harry sat down beside him.

"Have a drink," Jim said. "It'll take that disgustingly healthy glow off your face."

"I didn't realize it showed."

"Are you kidding? People are beginning to talk." Jim reached across the table to an ice bucket and retrieved a couple of cubes which he dropped into a plastic glass. "Care to name your poison, or shall I prescribe?"

"I gather I have a little catching up to do," Harry said.

"Let's put it this way," Jim said, "you're still in the starting gate and the rest of the field is entering the backstretch."

"Rum, then. With lime"

Jim filled the glass, squeezed a wedge of lime over it, and dropped the rind in. The golden liquid looked smooth and cool. Harry was suddenly thirsty. He took two long swallows and the back of his throat burned pleasantly from the spicy sharpness of the lime and alcohol.

Amid the general chatter around them, a single voice stood out, the words unclear but the persistent staccato tones evident through all other sound. As if reading Harry's mind, Jim smiled and said, "Hobie."

Harry nodded. "He never quits."

"He's not a bad old boy," said Jim. "Just gets a little garrulous when he drinks."

Harry smiled. "Where did you pick up a hundred-dollar word like that?

Jim took a swallow from his glass. "Hey, you're not the only guy around here with a fifty-plus word vocabulary." He reached for the bottle. "Anyway, I got it from you. See what setting a bad example can do? If you're not careful, you're going to end up educating the bunch of us."

Hobie's voice grew louder. "Who are those two guys he's talking to?" Harry asked. He was sure he had never seen the two dark-haired men in leisure suits who were uncomfortably trying to ignore Hobie.

"Oh Jesus," Jim said. "I didn't realize it was them he was talking to. Hope we don't have any trouble."

"What are you talking about?"

"That's the Orrik brothers. Levon and Henry. They own the funeral home up the street."

"Undertakers?"

"Yeah." Jim paused, then added with a smile, "Drinking bloody marys too."

"So Hobie's picking a fight with them because he doesn't like what they're drinking?"

"No, no. You see, they do some cremating work there now and then, and a few years ago we had a bad incident. Hobie and a couple of guys who aren't here anymore had just finished painting the topsides of a sixty-foot ketch. Hobie still claims it was the best job he's ever done. Unfortunately, the wind happened to be blowing straight out of the north that day and unfortunately those guys had a body in the furnace and unfortunately the furnace wasn't burning as clean as usual and unfortunately before you knew it Hobie and the boys had a sixty-foot white ketch that looked like somebody had dumped a giant ashtray all over the wet paint.

"Well, you know Hobie. He went crazy and took off for the funeral home waving his paintbrush and looking like Teddy Roosevelt going up San Juan Hill with the other guys right behind him.

"Apparently the mourners were still on hand when Hobie burst in, screaming at the top of his lungs that he was going to cremate the bunch of them and what did they mean blowing ashes all over the goddamn place.

"That was when Levon Orrik made the mistake of saying something. If he'd just kept quiet and tried to look mournful or something, everything might have ended right there. But no, Levon stands up in the front of the room and says he's the owner and what is the meaning of this intrusion on the grief of the bereaved for their lost loved one—or some such thing.

"The way I heard it, at that point Hobie just howled and started knocking over chairs and scattering the bereaved, grief or no grief, to all four corners of the room until he managed to grab

Levon by the throat. Everybody was shouting and screaming and crying and that brought the other guys with Hobie to their senses but not him. He was cursing a blue streak and slapping Levon around with his brush until Levon's face was as white as the ketch had been and then Hobie started dragging him over to the chute to the furnace.

"I don't know whether Hobie would really have pushed Levon down the chute because the other guys finally grabbed Hobie and dragged him out the front door.

"In the meantime, Henry Orrik had called the cops and everyone was screaming for Hobie's head. Luckily, the two cops who showed up were old friends of Jake's—and boat owners too, so you know whose side they took. The good ole boys stick together down here.

"Anyway, the cops managed to straighten everything out, mostly by threatening to charge the Orriks with interfering with lawful commerce or some such thing if charges were pressed against Hobie

"So the way it ended was Jake got Hobie to apologize for busting up the funeral and the Orriks promised to keep Jake informed about their cremation schedule so that he could plan paint jobs accordingly. But I don't think Hobie ever really forgave them for ruining that job."

"So now you think we're in for a replay of the brawl?" Harry asked when he had stopped laughing.

Jim smiled. "No, not really. Hobie will mouth off some, of course, like he always does about anything, but he knows if he ever started anything here in front of all our people he'd be out on his ear pretty quick."

"Can't be very pleasant for the Orriks, though," said Harry.

"No. But they give me the creeps." Jim shuddered and poured them both another drink.

Hobie's tirade continued only a couple of minutes before Jake adroitly defused it by calling him over to help with the oysters. Clever, Harry thought. Jake often played the dull-witted country boy but he was a lot sharper than he liked to let anyone guess.

The food was ready and after filling his plate Harry found himself a seat beside Cynthia Collins. She had dark hair and angular features and a deep tan that attested to the time and care she devoted to acquiring and maintaining it. Jake and his wife, Sophie, disapproved of Cynthia's fashion-consciousness and vanity but did their best to overlook these apparent flaws in her character for Junior's sake. As their only child and heir to his father's business and skills as a boat builder, Junior could do no wrong.

"Think you've got enough, Harry?" Cynthia asked, looking at the small mountain of food on Harry's plate and smiling.

"Oh, I don't know," he said. "This Florida air seems to give me quite an appetite. Besides, with what your father-in-law pays me I have to take advantage of every free meal I can get."

"What *are* you doing here, Harry?" Cynthia asked.

"You're the second person to bring that up today," he commented while spearing a chunk of deep-fried grouper with his fork.

"Who was the other?"

"Hobie Turner."

"Oh, God, him!" she said. "I'm serious, Harry. Why are you wasting your time around here? You could be doing anything. Living in New York. Or traveling. Imagine seeing Europe! All those places are just pictures to me. I sit around staring at magazines and you could be there."

"Why don't you and Junior go?" Harry asked.

"Because Junior thinks the world ends just outside Clearwater Bay. And also because we are both very married to this boatyard."

"Well, why didn't you go before you got married?"

"Money, for one thing. And I was too young to know any better. Did you know I married Junior when I was seventeen?"

"No, I didn't. That's awfully young."

"It's pretty normal around here, actually."

"Yes," Harry said, "I've noticed that. Kind of scary to see all these kids pushing baby carriages."

Cynthia nodded slowly, looking through glazed eyes at someplace or something far away. Harry wondered if he had blundered. She and Junior had been married seven years but had no children. Just as well, he thought coldly. If she feels as trapped as she sounds. But maybe that's part of the problem.

"Yes," she said softly, "there's a lot I'd like to see." She returned suddenly to the present and smiled. "Sorry. I drift off very easily when I get started thinking about these things. You still haven't answered my question."

"Well," Harry began, wondering how to explain or even if he should try, then deciding that she deserved an answer. "I know this is probably going to sound strange to you but one of the biggest reasons that I'm here is that I *have* seen Europe—or a lot of it—and I *have* lived in New York. I was born there and my folks still live there. If I'd done things differently—or maybe just not done a few things—I'd be working every day in a suit and tie in a glass tower on Madison Avenue, where the only things that actually get made are money and problems. Frankly, I like it better here." He wondered how to explain to someone who had never known anything else the comfort he found in small town life, the relief to be found in playing a role whose expectations were limited and clearly defined. "I like working outdoors and with my hands, and I like the feeling of accomplishment I get when I finish a job and can stand back and look at it. And I like being near the sea and boats. And I like the climate. And, most of all, I like the people."

Inadequate, he thought, as her face registered disbelief. "Really," he continued, "People here are part of something, and that something isn't so big that everyone's responsibility gets lost in the muddle. People here know who they are and what is expected of them and what to expect from each other. Look at tonight, for example. Look how everything got done without anyone having to be told what to do or made to do anything they wouldn't want to do. Everybody fits together like pieces of a puzzle. And if one of them were missing, somehow somebody else would fill in the missing piece." Cynthia still said nothing.

"Now," Harry said, "I'm not saying that other people— maybe you, for example—might not be happier somewhere else." She brightened considerably. "I'm just saying that for me, right now, there's no place I'd rather be than right here."

"You're a lucky man then, Harry," she said at last.

He nodded and smiled, lifting a steaming forkful of Nora Hanson's beans from his plate, and hoped she was right.

The rumble and clank of a tractor trailer truck coming through the boatyard's front gate caught his attention and like everyone else he turned to examine the boat being brought into the yard. A sleek, yellow racing sloop—Harry guessed of the One Ton class—but two or three seasons old and therefore distinctly uncompetitive in the ferociously contested sport of ocean racing for which she had been designed.

A blue Mercedes sedan with Connecticut license plates followed the truck into the yard. The owner, thought Harry. Down from the yacht club on Long Island Sound for a spot of fun on the Southern Ocean Racing Circuit. But why come all that way with an uncompetitive boat?

He had his answer in a moment. Emerging from the Mercedes, instead of the middle-aged stockbroker type he had expected, was the son of the middle-aged stockbroker type. He looked to be about twenty years old; was tall, blond, and lanky; and wore a maroon and white Harvard sweatshirt to go with a pair of faded jeans and boating moccasins. Another young man of similar type but darker coloring and wearing a blue sweatshirt with a "Y" on the breast, which Harry assumed stood for "Yale," got out of the car on the passenger's side. Two young women popped out of the back seat. They were both slim and, Harry thought, attractive in the kind of asexual way coed extras are, drifting about in the background of a film shot on location on a campus. They advertised no affiliations on their chests but they had the look about them of money and a pampered life.

So far, the four seemed not to have noticed the group of people eating not more than twenty feet from them. This was hard to believe possible unless their olfactory organs had been removed or altered in some way—which Harry thought just possible in the women, whose noses looked a bit too perfect. The four of them stared up at the boat resting on the trailer and chattered happily. Obviously they were eager to play with their toy. Suddenly, the brunette turned and smiled, as it happened, straight at Harry, and said simply, "Hello."

For no apparent reason, Harry felt terribly foolish and unable to speak. It was as if his throat had closed up completely. But his discomfort went unnoticed as almost everyone else responded with a greeting and Jake, smiling broadly, invited the new arrivals to "grab a plate and dig in." The truck driver walked happily over to the serving table where Jim Hanson poured him a drink. Harvard and Yale and the blond declined Jake's offer, despite the urging of the brunette. They had heard about a restaurant they wanted to try—but the brunette insisted she would stay. "I haven't come all the way to Florida to eat in a second-rate restaurant when I have the chance to sit outside by the water eating fresh fish and oysters." Harry smiled.

The Mercedes drove off and the newest guest was given a place of honor between Jake and Sophie. Harry watched her as she ate. He couldn't hear what she was saying but she was obviously enjoying herself and at ease with the situation and the company. It was her eyes, perhaps. Or the hint of amusement and perspective in her smile. Or the auburn tint in her hair now that she sat in the setting sunlight. Or a self-confidence that she would no doubt carry anywhere. Or some combination of them all. Or something else. Something.

When he had finished eating, Harry had a couple of drinks with Jim and they talked a bit about a thirty-footer they would be working on during the next week. It was getting late.

The floodlights were on. Harry was tired and a little tight. Harvard and Yale and the blond returned and the brunette said goodnight to everybody in general and left—with hugs to Jake and Sophie—and Harry decided it was time to go home. It bothered him momentarily that the two things might be related.

Nora Hanson agreed it was time to leave. Karen had already curled up and fallen asleep in the most comfortable chair she could find. Jim wanted to stay. He was having a fine time, he said, and could get a ride home from his old pal, Hobie.

Harry carried Karen to the Hansons' car and deposited her gently in the back seat, covering her with a light jacket of Jim's that he found there. He eased himself into the front passenger's seat. Nora smiled as they pulled out of the boatyard. "You ought to have one of your own," she said.

"Oh, cut it out," Harry said, laughing softly. "I think I'm more the uncle type."

"Bull," said Nora. "What you are is the chicken type. I saw you looking at that woman tonight."

"Jealous, huh?"

"You know what I mean. She *was* attractive."

"Sort of." Harry said.

"And you know what I realized?" Nora asked. "She's just your type."

"Nora, you think any woman is just my type," Harry said.

"I'm serious, Harry. That's why I haven't had any luck fixing you up. Your type doesn't exist around here."

"She and her friends are the kind of people I dislike most," said Harry.

"And the reason you hate them so much," Nora said, "is that you are one of them."

"No."

"I don't mean your values are the same, just your backgrounds."

"You're wrong, Nora."

"Come on, Harry. It was written all over you tonight. You took one look at those people and you knew them—or thought you knew them. But I think you were wrong about Sally."

"Sally?"

"I talked to her for a while and she's very nice. You can tell a lot about some people from even just a short conversation and she is definitely nice, not snooty like I know you think she is."

Nora pulled into the small parking lot outside the two-story house in which Harry had an apartment. "Stop kidding yourself, Harry," she said.

He leaned over and kissed her on the cheek. "You're crazy, Nora. Cute, but crazy. Goodnight. And I wouldn't wait up too late for that husband of yours."

"Don't worry. The only thing waiting up for him when he gets home will be the Alka-Seltzer bottle."

Harry laughed as she drove away. Jim let go this way about once a year and always ended up with a hangover that seemed to last for a week. But everyone needs something to repent.

His small apartment seemed even smaller than usual. He closed the door behind him irritably, knowing that he would not be able to sleep and annoyed that the evening had unsettled him. He poured himself a brandy and sat on the sofa in the dark living room. His body and head ached with a tense and unreasonable apprehension which was all too familiar, a persistent, dully throbbing dread like that of a fugitive, the more troubling because he was never able to identify its source. A nagging certainty that something was wrong, something that should be seen to urgently, but which lay just beneath the surface of conscious memory, maddeningly beyond reach.

There was Cynthia Collins to think about, trapped and frustrated and understandably eager to see the other side of the coin. And Nora—Nora and her perceptions. How close to the mark she had come it was hard to say, but she had drawn blood for sure, and from the feel of it, from some very old wounds. And he thought about the car from Connecticut and how he had considered its passengers trespassers, and how a chill had touched him for a moment, like an icy wind from someplace stark and unhappy.

He sat for a long time, and drank, and thought about many things. But he saw only one face.

Scott Anderson

— ((

The Passion of Saint Hayakawa

Saint Mary Hayakawa awoke to the sound of her own coughing. She fumbled for a match on the bedside table, and lit a candle.

Christ. There were lipstick stains on the cigarette ends in the incense burner. Too many of those and not enough deep breathing, that was her trouble.

What time was it? She squinted towards the balcony window, to see lights of ships on the Rio de la Plata, and nothing else. Still too dark, too early. Her bare feet flinched on the cold floor when she sat up. There was little hope of going to sleep now.

There, on the nightstand, was the tabloid headline: *Living Saint Escapes to South America,* and a photo of her in sunglasses, a floppy hat and a large raincoat, fleeing the camera like some peevish film star.

And what the Goddamn wouldn't they give for a picture of *this* moment, splashed across the front pages? What business was it of theirs, anyway? What did they expect, that she drank nothing but green tea? Without a little private sin to anchor her in place, she could be floating all over the globe—Greenland, Mongolia, the Ryuku Islands, God knows where else. Appearing in two or three places at once.

She liked Montevideo, for reasons that would make sense to no one else. It was a town that did not make a big show of religion—no patron saint, no shrines swarming with pilgrims. Christmas was known as Family Day. During Easter, people went to the beach or camping in the country instead of to Mass. She'd acquired a taste for mate'; there was a plentiful supply in Montevideo. Cinemas were cheap. And there were mountains, the Cuchilla Grande, albeit in the distance.

I am not afraid of discovery, she thought. Only misunderstanding.

She looked around the cave-like walls of her room. No television. A bed, a writing desk, the chest of drawers from Japan, a radio and CD player. The mirror and drapes were straight out of a motel room.

She remembered the tiny bottle of brandy saved from the Miami-Montevideo flight. It was tucked in a drawer of pocket-sized expense accounts and journals. She found it, unscrewed the cap, poured half a small juice glass full, and held it to the light.

Let us sing... Let us drink....

Where had she heard that? She looked through her small box of CD's for a clue.

Yes, here it was. The wedding chorus from Massenet's "The Virgin," the scene of the Wedding at Cana, when water was changed to wine. She put the disc on the player, and opened the sliding glass door. The strains poured into the night air. She sang with the refrain, confident she wouldn't be heard above the chorus.

En nous c'est une ardeur nouvelle
Gloire a Jesus! le Maitre des cites!
Fresh ardor pervades us
Glory to Jesus! The Master of cities!

She stepped onto the small balcony, squeezed between two bonsai plants and a pot of begonias. Colored light from neon signs on Misiones Street reflected in her drinking glass. She raised it, addressing the chorus to the thousands of souls in the capital city, some working, many more slumbering. She wanted to wake them, touch every last one with the music, shake them, if necessary.

Gloire le Maitre des cites! She took the liquid in three swallows. Tears came to her eyes. As she felt the brandy rolling down, she wondered what the chances were of it transmuting to orange juice before it crawled further through her stomach.

It felt much the same as her very first taste of alcohol. She'd filled her mother's silver wedding cup with dark red cooking wine for a ritual beneath her bedroom posters of goddesses Pallas Athena, Demeter, Sarasvati, and the Shinto deity Amateresu.

She remembered what she used to do when she was a girl and couldn't sleep. At the time when she'd first tasted the forbidden fruits of American magazines and candy cigarettes under the bedsheets, she'd written her first haiku.

Tucked far inside a top drawer in her dresser, she found an envelope that still held a few rice paper pages from grade school. She looked at one by candlelight.

> Moon kissing grass
> I speak kindly to the carp
> They will understand

Yes, she was sure they would, more than anyone else perhaps.

She slumped into a chair and closed her eyes.

At the Chuguji temple in Japan, she sat cross-legged for hours in meditation beside the garden pool. In the shallow water, between the rock arrangements, the koi, with their great whiskers and plated scales, drifted at the top of the water like cloth streamers in the wind. Their fins flashed at her while fireflies glided above the pool.

One by one they beached themselves on the shore. In the moonlight, their large eyes beckoned to her. She longed to reach out, to stroke them under their fins, but dared not break the stillness.

Eyes still closed, she lifted her nightdress. Her finger traced a circle around the spot just above her thigh. The nose, tail, and fin were still visible, though the hues of orange and blue, outlined in jet black, had faded since that painful night in a less than respectable neighborhood of Osaka.

It brought back all the old associations—vows of brother and sisterhood, late night political discourses, marches through the university, passion.

The cove in the shadows of Mount Fujiyama was the perfect spot, isolated from view, hidden from reporters, clergy, even her adoring family. While her mind sought absolute peace on the shore, her body rose and stepped into the gentle waves of Suruga Bay. Bare feet moved with ease on the sandy bottom. She walked into deeper green water, parting the long weed strands like the folds of a curtain.

A soft vibration, a shudder, rippled the water by her leg. She tensed, seeing a dark, sleek form approach. Sharks had been known in these waters. Then she saw the playful bobbing of a dolphin's head, like a child's toy, and returned to her state of grace.

One small eye turned up to greet her, and the nose casually brushed her leg. She saw her robe was floating about her waist, and felt shame.

The dolphin swam around her in a circle. Now it brushed far up her thigh. She realized that its nose was hovering about one particular spot: the small orange, blue, and black tattoo in the shape of a dolphin, etched across her thigh.

She made a deliberate effort to look into its eyes. Did it think she was in trouble?

Of course. Who else but a drowning human would be at these depths?

As the creature nuzzled her, she put out both hands to stroke its back. She traced a circle with her finger around its air hole, along the smooth line of its fin. With bowed head, it floated motionless beside her. She was unaware how many minutes, perhaps hours, she drifted with the dolphin in Mount Fuji's shadow.

There, if they still needed one, was a sign. A blessing from the animals, and she had been the only witness.

Another animal had started it all. It was in a mountain village above the Rio Oronoco, where she had been staying with a family in a flat box room with faded blue walls. She cradled a sick child who had just lost his cat. The cat lay in a basket, where it had gone to sleep the day before, never to wake.

If the cat couldn't get better, said the child, why should he? To help him sleep, Mary asked the boy to picture the cat as it had been in life, healthy and whole.

In the early morning, the cat sneezed, shook itself, and climbed out of the basket. The child recovered from his sickness. His mother ran to the neighbors, singing the praises of the good Sister Mary.

The documented signs accumulated from that time on. A spring in Colombia, thought to be dry and poisoned, gushed clear water three days after she had sat by it in meditation. A barren hillside grew fat with wheat not long after she'd sprinkled it with a handful of grain from Nepal. Travelers saw birds circling above her head as she walked down mountain roads.

By the time Sister Mary returned to her home convent on the Venezuelan coast, the Mother Superior had in her hands a thick pile of envelopes and reports, bound with string. She still had doubts about the young Sister who had come from the Buddhist monastery in Nepal, a recent convert to the Church. But after much prayer and reflection, Mother Superior decided to remove Sister Mary from her duties as general health practitioner and social worker at large, and channel her inspired energies into administration. From the Path of Service, to the Path of Paperwork.

After many seasons of careful observation and much prayer, Mother Superior penned a letter to the Episcopal Commission, whose domain was the investigation of miracles. Their reply urged secrecy, and further investigation, during which Sister Mary was shuttled from administrative position to infirmary to missionary work in the interior.

Three years later, she sat in a high-ceilinged Vatican room with painted blue clouds and Baroque angels watching above her. Somewhere in the vast Papal acreage, the Episcopal Commission secretly debated the candidacy of sainthood for Mary the Blessed, as she had come to be known.

She dismissed her anxieties about the debate, and permitted her mind to float beyond the Vatican walls as far as the ice-locked peaks of the Himalayas. She composed herself as tall and still and solid as a mountain, unattached to the outcome soon to be announced from the balcony over the Square of St. Peter.

The delegates from the Episcopal Commission found her sitting up, eyes open, but had to rouse her as if from sleep. When they knew she was with them, they bowed very low from the waist—the traditional Japanese greeting of deepest respect. There was no doubt that the petitioners of Santa Cecilia, the families, friends, and witnesses from a score of countries had triumphed over the dictum that the only fitting saint was a dead saint.

Vatican Scraps Millennium of Tradition was the headline in the English newspaper. And from that time on, from New Delhi to Tokyo, Miami to Montevideo, the lost week of airplane flights and public rituals, they hadn't given her a moment's rest. Accompanied by secret service and undercover Vatican officials (whom she couldn't tell apart after a while) she was escorted through downtown Montevideo to an unassuming church administrative building, conveniently located two blocks from the Cathedral. She was given the run of the top two floors. Rest was prescribed for her, and, eventually, a return to a working life.

The clamor of ships on the Rio de la Plata roused her. She stirred in her chair. It was light enough to see the clock by now. Eight a.m. Time to start the day like everyone else in the waking city. The hum of early traffic on the Rincon signaled the arrival of Monday morning.

What does a saint do for a living? The question never had to be asked before. Was it like that German saint of the early 1800's who had done nothing miraculous in her life but lie in bed and bleed profusely from her head and palms while writing down terrifying visions of the apocalypse?

She could easily spend her days writing in bed, telling stories to small children, bleeding discreetly, and blessing pilgrims who traveled from afar.

But there was her daybook, poking from beneath the tabloids on her nightstand. A calendar and pages full of lists, tasks to be drawn up, priorities to juggle. She had thank-you letters to write, some personal, some to be copied and printed on her new stationery. Her list of invitations included the Red Cross, the Pentecostal School, any number of orphanages, hospitals, and seminary schools to visit.

But troubling her most was the radio and television address she was expected to make. It would be carried live via satellite through every communications network the Church had access to. If there was one moment to sneak her first and last cigarette of the day, this was it.

A soft knock came on the bedroom door. "Your Grace?"

Mary stuffed the loose cigarettes into a lacquered box, and locked it. That was one decision that took no time to make. "Yes?"

"There is mail for you, Your Grace." The nuns and novices had a hard enough time living under the same roof with a saint, much less knowing what to call her. They had settled on "Your Grace."

"One moment, please." She fastened her morning robe about her, and opened the door to her office. The mail was piled on two desks. But her eyes went straight to the package against the wall at the far end of the room. It was a gray box, swathed in butcher paper, some of it peeling. Whatever was inside, the box itself, covered in the butcher paper, looked very old. The return address was Kinosake, her home town.

She undid the wrapping, which came apart easily in her hands. A thought stopped her. Did she have enemies? Not enemies, necessarily, but someone who would go as far as explosives to prove her sainthood?

The side of her that rested in the Vatican alcoves, in relics and simple faith, in absolute stillness on a cold floor in Nepal, said: the *hell* you will. She ripped the package apart.

Under layers of fine paper, there were old school books, letters, some in envelopes, some very old, bound in red ribbons. She peeked inside a bundle. The writing was her own.

164

Near the bottom was a framed picture: students, in sailor-style uniforms, the boys with their shirt tails out, the girls in uncomely dresses, standing with their bicycles in front of a cherry tree in full blossom. It didn't matter that the photo was faded black and white. She remembered the colors, the smell of damp earth on a spring afternoon, the feel of wind on her face.

She squinted at her face in the bathroom mirror. Wide awake and in complete control, but not above the call of the bladder and the growling stomach. She was always hungriest at this hour. With the thought of breakfast came the notion to do something really different today: stroll the main thoroughfare, take coffee at the Palacio Salvo Hotel, poke around the Mercado del Puerto for meat and vegetables while enjoying the street musicians. And she felt drawn to walk the mandala-like pattern that surrounded the statue at the Plaza Independencia.

Still, this was her first day of public Sainthood. She had the broadcast in the afternoon. At the very least she ought to attend morning service at the Cathedral, only blocks away, so long as there weren't crowds of pilgrims and the curious.

She wasn't yet ready for the intimidating numbers of people, reaching to touch her garment, looking into her eyes, beseechingly.

She shook the blur of alcohol remaining in her brain. Her mind felt as blank as the bare, dark walls of this room. It needed a new window. And on the walls, something with color. Perhaps a scarf, or a painted fan. Something in motion.

But was it allowed?

That question again. Would they understand? It would be asked again. What happens if a painted fan led to a hidden drawer, to nylons, concealed bottles, a little box full of cigarettes?

Saint Mary rummaged through the drawer for loose bills and change. In the drawer she found the sunglasses.

As she stepped out the side door of the church building, the concierge mumbled a greeting to the woman wearing dark glasses and an overcoat.

Along the Mercado, she found mate' and crusty bread. Strolling down the Rambla Roosevelt, chewing the last of her breakfast, she saw a vision encased in glass, and walked up to it.

It was a pair of carp, floating in water the color of Suruga Bay, behind the blue-green glass of a storefront aquarium.

"Motion, and color," she said aloud. She put her hands in the coat pockets and stepped inside to arrange the delivery of one large aquarium to the address at Misiones Street.

Lisa Starger

))

The Burned Girl

I don't remember how I heard about the burned girl. Probably it was my new friend Scot, with his spiritual leanings and whom I was seeing a lot of at that time, who told me. A new friend is useful in the kind of crisis that ensues when you are cutting your old life loose, or have had it cut loose for you. A new friend finds you starkly alone, sees you naked of attachment the way you cannot yet bear to see yourself. A new friend accepts you, even loves you, for your freedom, in a way that you realize you will have to come to, but cannot imagine how. My old friends felt like daggers then, pinning me to a shared history that was tearing painfully and an identity that was crumbling away.

The burned girl was so young, only nineteen or twenty, and had come to stay at the nearby Buddhist monastery. After she disappeared one night, a few of the monks had been delegated to search the adjacent autumn forest for a sign of her. They found a note under a rock at the base of a huge old tree, next to the charred remains of what was identified as her body. Apparently, she had drunk most of a bottle of wine and then with kerosene and matches, intentionally, unimaginably, set herself on fire.

Well, certainly it was shocking. And sad. And in the midst of my own ordinary troubles, I found myself thinking about her all the time. Night after night I put two worried children to bed with a look in my eye they had learned, I guess, to understand as meaning they had better not resist. I would open my nightly bottle of wine, settle in front of the TV, and instead of seeing whatever old movie or sordid sitcom was on the screen, I saw a young girl walking through dark woods. I pictured her as a very serious girl, wide-eyed under a shaven head. I wondered what she had revealed in her note. Had she done it all holy and fiery like some modern Joan of Arc, conceiving of her act as the only way to cut through the material matrix that bound her and go straight to God? I wondered, when it was begun, had she changed her mind?

Most of my mental energy was otherwise spent in an effort not to remember certain things I had heard (his tone of voice, a woman's breathy message on our machine), or seen (scented letters, hidden photographs), or even to think. If I let myself relax in any way, I was swamped with imagined visions of their lovemaking and an awareness of my abandonment that left me literally gasping like one drowning. My heartfelt intention to carry on as usual with everyday concerns was unsuccessful. Not surprising considering the minimal amount of cognitive force that was left free. I more than once found myself parked at the Grand Union unable to remember why I was there. Sitting in the car, plowed snow piled all around me, hours might pass before the cold or dark cut through my trance to remind me of buses unmet or children unfetched. Often I lost myself in thoughts about the burned girl. I watched her walking through the fall woods; the leaves so fragrant, the pine needles like spice, the soil dark and moist and sweet as if the coming winter had suffused all dying things with a last great intensity of essence and being. Had she noticed every tiny mushroom? Every birdsong noted and leading to the question, "Is that my last?" Or were her senses already withdrawn into herself and focused on that inner path to vast imaginary space? Did she hear a distant chainsaw marking someone's attention to coming need, or was her mind already out scouting ahead, gathering signs of the other world she was making for? Could she just have been trying to make somebody sorry?

The winter ground on, exceedingly small. Sometime in the middle of it I was informed, at some volume, over the telephone, after repeatedly insisting on being told the truth, that the person I had lived with for twenty years was happy with his new love, and did not intend to return. "So that's it," I repeated to myself, not very poetically. "So that's it," over and over like a mantra as if it settled everything and would point me marching toward my new life. But in reality, I was fastened to a post by a chain of refusal that dragged my purposeless steps around and around in a circle, wearing a rut so deep I forgot there was a world above my head.

And I thought about the burned girl endlessly, compulsively, even to wondering *why* I thought about her. I was twice her age at least, and tied to a life whose facts added up to nothing: no marriage, no job, no skills, and no sense of direction. The details of daily life were an external machine that marched me about to its own rhythm and requirements. And then, more disturbing than the feelings I had suffered in the midst of the initial pain, feelings whose intensity could not be stood for long, was the fear that dawned now—that this lifelessness could go on forever. There was nothing to stop it. I imagined the burned girl's face under the rigorous scalp; the luminous eyes seeing everything, the rare but glowing smile. I remembered that I had cut my hair drastically once, when just about her age. Home from college where I was failing classes and could not settle on a major, I began hacking away at my long hair with a vengeance born of self-loathing and the conviction that my life was at stake. Cutting away to uncover the core of me, the solid real center of something, I found nothing but an ugly appearance. Family members politely ignored the episode. I returned to school, buried myself in two more semesters, and then escaped the terror that was closing in on me by marrying my high school love.

As the cold weeks went by and my situation did not improve, I considered enrolling in one of the weekend retreats offered at the monastery. Even before I learned about the burned girl I had wondered what monastery life was like. I had read a little about it; early rising for sitting meditations, simple meals, simple work, more meditation, healing silences. I'd had a fantasy of being happy there.

169

But one day Scot mentioned offhandedly that, in his experience, there was a monk who would walk amongst the meditators and strike with a cane anyone whose attention seemed to be wandering.

When I was eight years old, my mother, hoping to smooth over my extreme physical awkwardness, enrolled me in a ballet class recommended by one of her friends. The teacher, an old bony woman with an indecipherable accent, had been a member of the Russian ballet, which supposedly excused her method of instruction. This method consisted of smart and unexpected whacks with a cane as well as verbal abuse directed at any girl assuming an incorrect or sloppy posture. I, predictably, was the most frequent recipient of the hateful, humiliating strokes. (Not only did I never learn any ballet, I refused to dance at all until college, when I learned to drink as well.) Scot's assertion shocked me enough that I looked no further into monastery matters.

One night in February, I awoke in a panic. I was accustomed to those dark hours of wine insomnia, but this was something different. What was going on? Even as I tried to remind myself that what I was afraid of had already happened, waves of panic began to build and my breath became shallower and shallower. I fought to breathe at all, convinced I was dying. Somehow, it was by thinking of the burned girl with her deliberate horrible purpose that I slowed the gasping and relaxed myself to sleep.

A thaw came in mid-March. It was impossible to tell if it was the real thing or one of those false starts that spring sometimes gives us. I conceived the desire to climb to the top of High Point Mountain, with some idea that I could breathe freely up there and shake off this thing that was strangling me from the inside. The trail was still fairly deep in snow and it took five hard hours of struggling to get to the top. Emerging onto a bald rock height, I saw the sky opened wide around me. The heat of the sun was surprising and I reeled a little. Giddily taking in the view, I was satisfied to see something that surprised and pleased me. Down in the valley, the landscape seemed all roads and stores, houses and wires—the forest all neatly parceled and tamed. But from the top of the mountain there was just one blanket of trees that stretched out in all directions, connecting everything. There was enough coniferous forest that even at the end of winter this was so. "The monastery would be about there," I thought, looking west, "and my house over in that direction." I traced my finger in a line to the east. It was one forest connecting those two places. And, somewhere in between, the place where the burned girl died. The trip down was much easier than going up had been, but for days I ached from the unfamiliar exertion. It felt good to have real physical pain to contain me.

In April, I went into the woods. I can place the date exactly on the fourth because the third had been my daughter's seventh birthday and after sleepwalking through her party like I did everything else, I had arranged for her and her brother to stay with friends. By the time I finished packing a satchel with a sleeping bag, a notebook and pen, a bottle of Merlot and an opener, some matches and a small bottle of kerosene, it was late afternoon. The woods were already soft and darkening when I walked in by the trail behind my house. In no time at all it was too dark to see, so I wrapped myself in the sleeping bag and sat at the foot of an old pine, on the side out of the wind. I was surprised how comfortable I felt. The sound of the wind stirring the branches of the trees just added to my sense of security. I opened the wine and took a long draught out of the bottle. A wave of emotion hit me, so foreign and unexpected and mixed. There was real joy in it, like I couldn't remember ever feeling and maybe had only read about. There was sadness too, heavy, heavy sadness and an achey, stretchy feeling like something in my chest was changing shape and breaking apart in the transformation. I poured out some kerosene onto a small pile of twigs and leaves. The light shot out all gawky angles and shadows when I lit the match, as if the fire had changed the shape of the world around me. Comfort was banished as presences seemed to move at the perimeter of the light. I wanted to touch the burned girl. I didn't know her name, I didn't know anything about her I hadn't imagined, except the way she chose to die. Maybe I wasn't dying, but it was by default only and by way of some stubborn blind persistence that didn't feel anything like being alive. I wrote her this, and what I imagined she felt. I wrote what we might have said to each other had we met with open and knowing hearts. I wrote how angry I was that she had thrown away the youth I wanted back. I poured out my regret, imagining myself at home that night, all unknowing and self-absorbed, while not far away she entered the forest alone. I tried to describe how I felt like her double and her mother and her child, all at the same time. I mailed the letter by burning it a page at a time in the fire.

The burned girl didn't seem like Joan of Arc to me now, just small and lost and scared. I watched her in my mind's eye as the whole world receded from her in some terrible tide that had no return, but receded forever. I cried for her, and in my tears felt I had found her in that bright and dark place. I felt myself go to her and hold her while she burned, believing she would somehow know that I had put my own burnt heart next to hers and there, in the fire, loved her.

Simone Felice

))

Out the Train Window

For a long while there had been a highway running parallel to this railroad and alongside the highway the million telephone poles that have from day one promised always to keep us in touch but have they kept us in touch?

I can see farmland.

Now with the highway gone, the poles for the most part gone, everything I see is farmland and with it the living backdrop of the sky.

Now through the slightly dirty and moving frame that is the train window I am able to view, not far off, a small house and on the lawn is someone's daughter bringing down laundry from a clothesline. At this distance one could never see the clothespins but one knows them to be there between her fingers just the same.

Her movements are soft. Deliberate. Like those of someone who has walked a long time alone in the woods and has become aware to the notion that there is in fact a living world outside the manmade one. She folds the random textiles and lets them fall into the basket at her feet.

How would it be to fall in love with that girl and exist out here in the interior? To listen for the train at intervals and then watch it pass. A thing that should seem so wholly alien out in this place but does not. Its whistle and the riot of its coming and going common in the night. Outside. Herself and myself underneath this quilt. Inside. My farmgirl fast asleep against me. Her body smelling as authentic as a body can. The sound of her breathing in the bedroom being the most beautiful metronome the worldwide.

I am not asleep. The train is passing. It comes and it goes away. The train is passing out there on the flats but I am coupled here with my love. It will not take me away never take me away with its promise of soon delivering its living cargo somewhere but in the end delivering it nowhere. She is breathing in the bedroom and I am not. No, she is outside in the last light of the day taking everything down from the clothesline and I am on the train seat half a mile away and half delirious watching her figure and the figure of the house grow small and small and she has no idea who I am.

Out the train window we are witness only to whatever truths the Americascape might be willing to share with us. All of her beautiful or maybe terrible algebra which lives and has lived in every tree, under all the rivers and inside every bird's stomach long before the boats came. So long before we plugged everything into the wall. But since this all has come to pass it would be unfair to say that her algebra has not been subsequently modified. Modified forever.

~

To wake in another part of the country without ever moving one's feet seems to me a felony against the very way we've been made.

I suppose I dreamt and in that dream I heard, more than once, my own self crying out for mercy from a thousand miles away. And though I could not see this twin otherself long across that dark expanse of land I knew that it was naked and tied to a chair. I knew also that the screamer was me and not me but some secret refugee come smuggled out of my mother's belly in the same minute as me and once this far lifeform had been young and once it had been free but at one time so had we all.

The sun has begun its rising through the darkness outside my window. Showing itself in its slight and tested way like a thin virgin standing inside of her thin slip against the bedroom door.

Half of her visible, half of her lost, wishing not to reveal too much of what she is at once and so too has it always been with this same speculate wonder that men have waited for the coming of the sun.

Now in the half light there on the grasslands I am moved, in a way, to see rising out of the ground what I know not to be dinosaurs, of course, but here in this small and palsied hour of the morning their goliath shapes seem to own all the look of those animals and animalbirds who had long before any Eden been the sovereigns of this earth until whatever it was that took them away took them away.

But what I see out there in silhouette are no dinosaurs. The train and me inside the train are beginning to pass them now and I can see them for what they are. What the oilmen call the pumpjacks. The oilfields. See them. Down and up and down and up again, halfliving in their limited animea. Lonesome idiot heads, bobbing monstrous against the red sky behind. Pledged to one thing: the harvest of all fossils and fuel from out of that hard uterus under the world.

And I can see it as no light irony that these machines might have come to be shaped this way. Chance replicas of the very animal whose bones and sap have been stolen by this empire to make this empire what it is. And it is yet to be seen if the oilman and all his people might one day suffer the same end or perhaps a sister end. With these dead bones of ours as the chief component in a new and golden fuel made light and thin to propel god knows what with god knows what at the wheel. Though it does not seem to be within our relentless blueprint ever to completely die away.

Oil. Black gold.

And there are some that might remember another black gold upon these shores at one time though not a time out of mind. A black gold that would weep and fall in love with one another and sing a music soft in the twilight. It seems the podiums have all been torn away but the auction has never really ended. The one has replaced the other (as the boy flag bearer will bend to hold up the tattered burden of his dead confederate and what a burden it is, though the boy, the quick and the dead, will never see the true reason for his being on that battlefield, he sees the colors and the chrome and it pours a love into his heart and for that alone he is beautiful and young forever). The one has replaced the other and the auction finds itself at the gas station these days with the numbers fluctuating overnight under the quiet and cover of dark. Funny how the rise and fall of pennies can affect the way we feel about a given day. But the pump fits so nice into the orifice of the Ford or whatever. Sex has always sold but not sex alone. The pump itself being shaped not only like our male member but also like our hand-held revolver and where would we ever be without that duo?

I can't see the oil fields through the window anymore, only the land. And here I am convinced that if I could ever believe in America it would be only her wild blood that I'd believe in, not her banner never her banner no matter how broad the stripes, how bright the stars; her bad art on a tablecloth to which we've attached everything that we are, everything that we might someday be. And how could those stars ever be expected to endure stitched on in their one dimension with never a chance to burn as does their myriad namesake all over the night sky. But maybe they will have their moment to burn because isn't it in the nature of the star itself to burn out and fall down when its time has come? Fall in that dark theatre and in this one? Fall without protest because of the knowing in its middle that there is and will be an order to things.

~

It is September outside, I believe, though I'm not sure. And this engine has brought me to the coastline. Two seabirds circling one another there above the water with nothing but the wind and the motive of wind to choreograph. The beauty aside, there seems to be some pressing trouble upon the hearts of these birds and though the trouble is for those hearts alone, I think I feel it here in my own body because I too have known how it is to be that way.

A man is running up and down the beach with a small girl, both of them holding in their hands a bundle of string tethered to the kites above. One yellow, one deep red.

A good distance down the coast is an old lighthouse wasting away with all or most of its windows gone. The lamp is dead. Not long before dark it had begun to rain and now it is falling hard. I would love to stop this train and jump out into the sand and with my own hands and a few simple tools somehow bring a life once more into the lighthouse. So that there might be some beacon for the lost to follow in all the dark. But I haven't got it in me. I can not stop this engine no more than I can stop the rain against the windows. But I know soon there will come a softer rain to follow after the downpour—with only a brief intermission between—so that the world might have a blue moment of rest. A small time to be alone and broken hearted.

Listening to Music
(Thomas, Elizabeth, & Tani)
Carol Field

Contributors

Ty Adams, a playwright, won the Grand Prize from the Contemporary Arts Center in New Orleans for his first play, *The Camel Shepherds*. In New York, his plays have been produced by the Irish Arts Center, The New American Theatre, The WestBank Cafe, The Director's Company, and Circle Rep. His radio noir play, *Save Me*, was broadcast on NPR. He teaches writing in the summer at Southampton College, is a fine art photographer, and is currently co-owner of a bed and breakfast in Woodstock.

Scott Anderson is a not-too-recent émigré to upstate New York from Los Angeles, where he tried his hand at screenwriting and was a member of Artists' Repertory Theatre in West Hollywood. His recent writing credits include *Chronogram* and *Communities* magazines. He has read poetry both at local venues and the Festival of the CoffeeHouse Poets in Ontario. He wrote the scripts and performed in a recreation of a golden age radio program, *The Adventures of Marjorie*. His writing group, known as "The Glaring Omissions," has given a number of readings in the Hudson Valley.

Deborah Artman's fiction reflects a background that includes music, theater, poetry and film. She was recently awarded a 2002 New York Foundation for the Arts Fellowship in Fiction, and she is currently working on a novel to be published by Harmony Books in 2004. Deborah frequently collaborates with artists in other media and recently wrote the libretto for *Lost Objects*, an oratorio by composers Michael Gordon, David Lang and Julia Wolfe, which premiered at the 2001 Dresden Music Festival in Germany and was released on CD by Atlantic Records.

Holly Beye writes stories, and she writes plays that get produced in off-off Broadway houses in New York and on the West Coast. She also writes poetry, performs with the Comets Acting Troupe, and demonstrates for Peace, which may be the most important thing she does.

Audrey Borenstein's fiction has appeared in a variety of literary publications since the 1960's. She also has published essays, poetry and manuscripts of her Journal writings, five books of nonfiction, and a chronicle of local history. Her book, *One Journal's Life*, was published in 2002 by Impassio Press in Seattle. Borenstein's awards include an NEA Fellowship and a Rockefeller Humanities Fellowship. "Tomorrow's Work" is adapted from a literary novel she completed, an exploration of alternate lives in the Mid-Hudson Valley in a community founded in the 17th century by French Huguenots.

Thomas H. Brennan lives in Garrison, NY, and writes anywhere he can. His book *Writings on Writing*, a reference work for writers, was first published by McFarland and reprinted by Barnes and Noble. His stories have been published by *The Griffin, The Barkeater, Fan—A Baseball Magazine*, and *The Independent Review*. He is seeking a publisher for the second volume of *Writings on Writing*. He is a member of the Hudson Valley Writing Center in Sleepy Hollow and the FlashFiction workshop online. He thanks all his writer colleagues.

Barbara Brooks began writing fiction a few years ago, after leaving the chaos of Manhattan for the relative peace and quiet of Armonk, NY, where she now lives with her husband, two-year-old son, teenage stepdaughter and three noisy dogs. She has been a publicist and communications writer for twenty years, and will soon complete her M.F.A. at Bennington College while working as the marketing director at Manhattanville College. "Girls and Women..." is her third published short story.

Edward M. Cohen's novel, *$250,000*, was published by Putnam; his non-fiction books by Prima, SUNY Press, Prentice-Hall and Limelight Editions. He has published over 20 stories in such journals as *Harrington Gay Men's Fiction Qrtly, James White Review, Thought*, and won Honorable Mentions in the Lorian Hemingway Story Contest, Arch & Bruce Brown Foundation Short Fiction Contest, and Evergreen Chronicles Novella Contest. He lives in West Park and is currently completing a new novel.

Al Desetta lives in Woodstock, NY, with his wife Leah and son Joshua. He taught writing to teenagers, incarcerated youth, and young people in foster care for many years. He was founding editor of a national, award-winning magazine for foster youth. He has edited books on resilience, bereavement, and mental health issues for teens. He has been previously published in The Minnesota Review.

Bob Dunne is a member of the faculty at Yale University. He lives in the village of Cornwall-on-Hudson with his wife, Marguerite Dunne, the herbalist, and Ra, the cat.

Simone Felice is a writer, poet, and musician living and working at his Palenville home in the Catskill Mountains. He has been published in journals internationally and has performed his work all over Europe and America, appearing on BBC Radio (London) and featured at The Nuyorican Poets Cafe (New York) and the Black Box Theater (San Francisco). *The Big Empty*, his band, will have released it's self-titled debut album on December 13, 2002 (Superstar Label). His first book of poetry, *The Picture Show*, was published in 2000 by HUNGER Press. See http://simonefelice.ghod.org.

Carol Field is a visual artist who lives and works in Ulster County. Her work has been exhibited in New York, California, and Europe. The images here are from an on-going series of small drawings done in postcard format, spontaneous notations inspired by a night of good music, the flight of fireflies, the undulating horizon-line of a good hike. Her work is informed by an intimate connection with nature and the environment around her, and her past working experiences in creating vast paintings and set designs for MTV, Nickelodeon, VH1, Showtime, and other film, commercial, video, and theatrical productions.

Donald Ray Gilman grew up in the swamps of Louisiana. Son of a New Orleans prostitute, he moved from foster home to foster home most of his childhood. He is currently writing a screenplay based on those experiences. "My Panther" is based on "snapshots" from his memories. After moving to New York City, he worked as a bartender, an actor, a propmaster, and now a Multimedia Producer. He lives in Saugerties with his wife and son. He hopes that his work honors the teachers, social workers and other angels who showed up every time...just in time.

Scott Maxwell grew up outside of Rochester, New York. He graduated with an Associate degree from Adirondack Community College. Currently he is living in Rosendale with his girlfriend Leah.

Irene McGarrity lives in New Paltz and spends her time pacing at two-and three-hour intervals in her apartment, involved in dialogues with herself of great existential importance. She also composes poignant and compelling songs on her acoustic guitar, which are often inspired by her stories. Some titles include: "Kiss Me You Rubber-Faced Fool," "Mamma Wears the Pants in This Here Family," and "Dead Mice Are a Serious Vice." She lives with her turtle Pookie, who is allowed to keep as many dead insects in his tank as he likes.

Dina Pearlman has been involved with the arts since she first gripped a crayon in her native Massachusetts. After momentary stints as a rock musician, modern dancer and a professional photographer, she has primarily concentrated on exhibiting her visual art and writing and performing her poems and short stories. She's read at the Poetry Project at St. Mark's in New York City, and was featured at The Woodstock Poetry Festival as well as other venues throughout the Hudson Valley. Her work has appeared in numerous publications including *Triangle Shirtwaist Fire, Chronogram, Dyed-in-the-Wool, Wildflowers,* and the *Half Moon Review.*

Brent Robison makes his living as a multimedia writer/producer. He won a 1995-96 Fiction Writers Fellowship from the New Jersey Council on the Arts, and has published short stories in *re:Issue, Alchemy*, and *Crania.* An '80s immigrant to the NYC area from Utah, he followed love north to the Catskills, and now lives with his wife, sculptor and maskmaker Wendy Klein, on the far western edge of Woodstock.

Maia Rossini lives in Rifton, NY, with her husband and son. She is a producer for *Hipmama.com* and *Mamaphonic.com.* She received her MFA in Creative Writing from The New School University in 1998.

Kate Schapira has just completed the first draft of her first novel. Her stories and poems have appeared in several paper and e-publications. She teaches writing at the Astor Home in Rhinebeck and is scheduled to teach U.S. Women's History in Camp Beacon Correctional Facility, beginning in December 2002, thanks to an AAUW grant. She recently moved across the Hudson, from Germantown to Kingston, and is happily exploring her new surroundings.

Lisa Starger is a fiction writer, poet, comic strip artist, and teacher. Her work has appeared in *Chronogram* and various editions *of The Woodstock*

Poet's Anthology, as well as *Archae* and *Satori* magazines. After travels in Europe, Egypt, Malaysia, Hong Kong, and China, she settled in Olivebridge, where she dreams of living on a houseboat.

Fred Stelling is a full-time stay-at-home Dad and part-time Realtor living in Newburgh, where his beautiful wife supports him as he pursues his writing muses. His career in the medical field spanned over 20 years. Fred has a degree in Public Relations, and has written several technical articles for medical publications. "Electricity" is his first published work of fiction.

Jasmine Tsang was born in Shanghai. She was a student editor of the Sunday Examiner in Hong Kong. She graduated from St. John's University, did part-time guide work in the UN, and received her MA from Vassar. She also taught at Bennett College and Dutchess Community College. Her writing has appeared in *Short Story International, CAAC Inflight magazine, Dutchess Magazine, The Country, Westchester Family*, and *Hudson Valley Mature Life*. Last fall, Andover Green published one of her children's stories. "The Visit," an excerpt from her novel *A Concubine for the Family*, was a winner in the Hudson Valley Talespinner Contest.

Valerie Wacks is a real estate attorney in Ulster County. Her poetry has been published in *the Subterraneans, Voices of Selene, Echoes of Avalon*, and *In Country*. She is currently revising her second novel whilst her first novel wanders forlorn in search of a publisher.

Tania Zamorsky worked for years as a staff attorney at the non-profit Authors Guild, Inc., where she helped authors with their legal and business affairs. She is currently working as a freelance editor/writer while pursuing her own creative writing. Tania lives near Woodstock. "Squid in Love" (the title, though not the tale, inspired by the name of an entrée on a Thai restaurant menu) is her first published story.

Thanks to Wendy,
the essential element in my world